Shots in the Dark

The crack of a rifle, followed instantly by a tinkle of breaking glass, raised the hackles along Hastings' neck and sent shivers down his arms. He grabbed the lamp with his left hand and chopped at the chimney with his right, shattering the glass and extinguishing the light. Throwing himself to the floor, he rolled away from the table and lay motionless for a moment, letting his eyes adjust to the dark. Slowly he got to his feet and edged silently through the dark interior of the cabin to the door. His hand found the latch and lifted it.

Jerking open the door and palming his six-gun, he lunged into the inky blackness. A flash of lightning outlined briefly a black, shadowy figure rising out of the mud, gun in hand. Hastings' gun bucked in his hand. Once! Twice! Had he been shooting only at an image impressed on his vision by the brief flash of light? Had he hit his adversary?

Another bolt rent the darkness. Hastings sloshed his way toward the place where he had last seen the shadow. His foot struck an obstacle, and he leaned over, straining his eyes.

A body lay face down in the mud.

DENTON'S ARMY

RALPH D. CROSS

LEISURE BOOKS ∞ NEW YORK CITY

A LEISURE BOOK

Published by

Dorchester Publishing Co., Inc.
6 East 39th Street
New York City

Printed in the United States of America

1

The lone rider urged a lathered black horse through a shimmering veil of baking heat laced with a haze of powdery dust. An attempt to moisten cracked swollen lips resulted in his dry tongue sticking in place like paper backed with spirit gum. He removed a sweatstained hat and slapped it against his thigh, sending little flowery puffs of dust blowing away. An arm drawn across his forehead came away with a muddied layer of sweat and trail dust. He tugged at a large pie-tin canteen slung loosely from his saddle cantle. A large container, obviously homemade, it consisted of two large pie tins crudely soldered together with a strip of tarnished metal in between, giving breadth to the canteen. It was topped with a spout of sorts, stoppered with a large bottle cork. The man pulled, and the cork came out with a muffled pop; a piece of it crumbling away in his hand. He tilted the canteen and took a long pull of the tepid water, flavored with a subdued metallic taste.

The trail ahead wound through dry, brown grass and disappeared beyond the next rise. The trail behind him was long. Yet it seemed like only yesterday that he had left the secluded neutral sanctuary of the Nations.

"We've been on the trail for sometime now, ole fellow,"

he said to the horse as he patted its sleek neck. "I know it ain't been an easy ride, but that gent might just be here. We ain't looked this far north before. Of course, that job may be filled by now, but we ain't worried none about that—are we, ole fellow? We'll check to make sure. Earnin' wages might be enough of a reason to stay around until we've had a look-see."

The horse whickered and shook its head as if it had understood all that its master had said.

The man's mind drifted back to a day many years ago. A day much like the present one except the infernal dryness of the air had been lacking. Bitterness welled up within him as it did each time he recalled that day. With considerable effort he forced his thoughts back to the present. It wasn't likely the man would be here anymore than he was in the countless other places he had looked. Twenty-one years were a long time, and he had seen him only on the one occasion, but the image was still clearly etched in his memory. The nameless man may have drifted west but, just as likely, he could be back East somewhere. Yet the cruel, sadistic nature of the amoral creature that had been at loose on the Hastings's Plantation that day was more akin to the West, so he had been seeking him in bustling frontier towns which seethed with people of his moral bent. Each time the possibility of finding him arose, he faced the situation with a fatalistic view. More than likely the man was back East somewhere, the memory of the episode that had provided the impetus for the present course of the rider's life tucked away in a corner of his brain and all but forgotten. Maybe, deep down, he didn't really want to find him.

The horse topped a rise, and Bret Hastings pulled up short in the saddle. A lean, brown hand held the reins lightly, and one long leg dangled free of the stirrup. Before him lay a broad, shallow valley resting sedately between two hummocks of rolling prairie—a ribbon of green in an otherwise brown grass-covered landscape. A sluggish, umber stream wound its way from the north to join an unseen river somewhere to the south. Nestled along the stream about a mile from his vantage point was a town; a cluster of nondescript, sod and frame buildings, hidden by false fronts; some freshly painted, some with paint peeling, and others showing only bleached, gray wood too long exposed to the sun. This was Northgate, the town he was seeking.

The word had reached out from Northgate and filtered over the prairie from town to town, finally reaching him in a temporary sanctuary in the hills of the Cherokee Nation not far from the capitol, Tahlequah. The message had said that one Frank Slater would pay prime wages for a bodyguard, with a special assignment to be specified upon hiring. Out of curiosity he had responded immediately and now he was here.

Hastings nudged his horse lightly with a heel and began the descent down the trail. The town lay in the shape of a *T* with one street paralleling the river, and a single leg, framed with false-fronted buildings forming the base of the *T* and pointing west—the direction from which he was approaching.

He pulled his steed to a halt in front of a saloon—one of several—and patted the horse's quivering, lathered neck and slid from the saddle. Eyeing the front of the newly white-washed building, he let his eyes shift first to his right, assessing the town up to the main cross section with a glimpse of the river in the background, then to his left, shifting his gaze to glance back up the dusty trail over which he had just rode. His right hand snaked down and gently lifted the pistol part way out of the tied-down holster, then dropped it gently back to its resting place.

Splashed across the front of the building before him in

7

bold, black script were the words: Slater's Saloon.

Moving cautiously forward, his eyes shifting from side to side, he surveyed and catalogued his surroundings. The street was deserted except for an old man rocking serenely on the porch of the hotel on the river side of Slater's. The man was quickly dismissed as no significant threat to his well-being. Slowly, he mounted the steps as if trying to put off the encounter with Slater. Just as he was about to push through the batwing doors of the saloon, he caught a flicker of movement off to his right, toward the river. He turned, his hand hovering over the butt of the holstered pistol. The movement proved to be a man on a large white horse which was plodding unconcerned around the corner.

The rider was tall with abnormally long, thin legs, giving an appearance of being too long for the horse. The newcomer was slumped in the saddle, shoulders hunched forward. A flat-crowned, broad-brimmed hat was pulled down to eyebrow level. A frilly lace-fronted shirt was visible beneath a brilliantly brocaded vest which, in turn, was partially hidden by a black swallowtail coat.

Even at this distance he had no trouble recognizing Tucker Johnson. As Johnson approached, he let his hand lightly brush the walnut handle of his Colt, ready for whatever ensued—and knowing Johnson, that might be anything.

Johnson's head bobbed slightly with the motion of the horse. His eyes appeared to be closed as if he were deep in thought or sleeping as he rode. To the casual observer it might appear that Johnson was indeed lost in slumber and totally unaware of his surroundings, but it was nothing but a facade, ingeniously contrived, for the act had served its purpose numerous times. Many a man had been fooled by this fakery and, attempting to take advantage of Johnson's apparent nonconcern with his

8

surroundings, had found himself on the slow end of the draw—the advantage turned with no way to get it back. More often than not that gent learned a lesson that came too late while his life oozed out through bullet holes neatly placed by Johnson's marksmanship.

It had been over four years since he had last seen Johnson. The last time had been in Kansas City. Stopping at a saloon for a drink, he had noticed Johnson, whom he hadn't known at the time, deeply engrossed in a poker game. There had been three others at the table, two of which could have been local business men or professional gamblers—well dressed by any standard. The third had been dressed like a drover with faded flannel shirt tucked into batwing chaps. Somehow, to Hastings, the cowboy didn't fit the image. Curiosity had risen, sparked by an aura of the unusual that surrounded the game. He had sat a few tables away, nursing a beer, most of his attention directed toward the game but, out of habit, a part of him had kept surveillance over the rest of the room. His position had been selected with care, his back to the wall. He clutched a stein of frothy beer with his left hand, his right rested lightly on the table.

As he watched, Johnson continued to win far more than he lost. The stacks of coins before him grew with amazing regularity. Most amazing was the fact that this fellow was winning despite the appearance of being half asleep. He was slumped in a chair with eyelids drooping and fluttering as if he were desperately fighting sleep. There was a spark of excitement in the smoke-blue air. Trouble was coming!

The drover, over a period of time, had cautiously removed a pistol from the pocket of his chaps and placed it in his lap. The pot had been building rapidly, and one by one the players dropped out until only Johnson and the cowboy were left. The game came to an abrupt end when the cowboy tossed in the rest of his stake and called. Johnson dropped his cards and raked in the pot. The cowboy's hand had been good but not good enough. His face reddened as he saw he had lost all he had to the sleepy scarecrow across the green-topped table.

"You cheat!" the cowboy shouted, leaping to his feet and shoving his weight against the edge of the table while at the same time bringing his gun up in one swift movement to point at Johnson's chest.

Johnson pushed back slow from the table, clearing his ivory-handled revolver for action. The gambler was calm and confident.

Hastings watched three burly men, resembling miners more than cowhands, move away from the bar with guns drawn. His eyes followed them briefly, then flipped back to the drover in time to catch a sly signal from the cowboy to the three who now stood behind Johnson. Johnson, about to rise, had also seen the signal despite the fact that it had been extremely quick and well disguised. He settled back into his chair.

The cowboy issued a gloating laugh, holstered his gun, produced a canvas bag from somewhere within his chaps, and began to scoop up the money from the table. He walked toward the bar situated behind Johnson. A near-sighted old man partially blocked his path. The old man tried to move aside, but he was too slow to suit the cowhand. Jerking his pistol aloft, he brought the barrel slashing down across the old man's head. The old miner crumpled to the floor, blood gushing from a four-inch gash in his scalp. The cowboy stepped over him as if he were no more than a broken chair and emptied the till under the bar. Once again he drew his gun and leveled it at no one in particular. As he backed toward the door, he was joined by his three friends.

Draining his beer mug, Hastings watched Johnson rise

slowly, arms hanging limply at his sides. It was obvious that the lanky gambler was going to force a play! Not waiting to weigh the odds, he rose and slipped quietly to Johnson's left so that about fifteen feet separated him from the lanky gambler. If Johnson was aware of his entrance into the play, he gave no sign. Gambling that Johnson knew he was there and taking his side, he surveyed the situation, gauging his chances and theirs against the retreating quartet. He decided on a course of action, hoping that Johnson would read the situation the same as he. He directed his attention toward the two thieves on his left, trusting the gambler to go for the two on the right. He couldn't be positive that the gambler would draw on them but he was staking his life on it.

The fight had come almost unexpectedly. A barrage of shots split the silence. He had not even been conscious of Johnson's move, yet, one instant Johnson had been standing there in a slouched, limp position, and the next he was crouched and firing. Their moves had been simultaneous; there had been no exchange between them, no signal, yet the action had been initiated as if on cue.

As the smoke cleared Johnson assumed his old, sleepy pose. He stepped over the four outstretched bodies, picked up the canvas bag, counted out a sum of money, pocketed it, and tossed the bag to one of the others who had been at the table with him. Johnson had glanced at him, said nothing, yet the invitation had been clear. He had followed the gambler to the door, not sure of where it would lead him or why he was going along.

Outside the night had been cool, and the sparkling stars were bright. They had ridden west. Two weeks they had ridden together, and he had found in that time that Johnson could be likeable at times and that he would do things—almost anything—for money. Gambling was one exception to his general outlook on life. A bet was the one

11

thing he held sacred—win or lose, a bet had to be honored. Gambling was apparently the only religion Johnson knew.

A loner until his two weeks with Johnson, Hastings had soon grown tired of his ways, and they had parted company. Johnson had gone on to Colorado and he had headed into New Mexico Territory. That had been four years ago.

Now, as he stood at the door of Slater's, he knew he had a rival for the job if it were still available. Johnson would fight for it, and he merely wanted to satisfy an aching curiosity, an ache not worth fighting about. He could back out—let Johnson have it. But, no, that wouldn't do. Johnson mighty just take it as a sign of weakness and push into a fight anyway.

"Howdy, Bret-boy," Johnson said in a voice that sharpened his awareness of the gambler. Watching the lanky character dismount he kept a hand close to his holstered gun.

"Hello, Tuck. It's been a long time."

"Sure has, compadre. What brings you to this section of the country? I always thought you was southern in your ways." He chuckled. "You want that job, I bet. Well, Bret-boy, you've just been bested. Ole Slater wants the best his money can buy, and he cain't buy no better than Tucker Johnson!" The tone was jovial, but Bret knew that he was dead serious.

"Now, I'll buy a drink fer old times sake, then you fork yer hoss, Bret-boy, and ole Tuck'll show Slater that his luck is changed. I don't want any hard feelings but I need that money right bad, Bret-boy!"

"Like hell you do," Hastings growled in a similar jovial tone, mocking Johnson. "You should pay Slater for the chance to work for him—anybody as slow and sleepy as you are." Hastings chuckled. "Too damn bad, now ain't it

Tuck, but I got here first, and that counts for somethin'."
He watched Johnson closely, his hand hovering over his
gunbutt, knowing the chances of both of them walking
through that door were not good.

"Well, now," Johnson said. "You did at that, but you
haven't braced Slater about his proposition. Now, maybe
you got here first, Bret-boy, but ole Tuck is gonna talk to
Slater first. You want to argue?" Johnson climbed the
steps slowly, hardly stretching his long legs to take them
two at a time, and stood next to Hastings.

"We'll see," Hastings said. Two choices faced him:
Mount up and ride or prepare to take his chances with
Johnson. For the first time that he could remember, he
had to win and he wasn't sure that he could. "Let's have a
drink and talk it over." To his surprise, Johnson
complied.

The interior of the saloon was dim and as deserted as
the street outside. They stood just inside the door for a
moment, waiting for their eyes to adjust to the dim
interior, then they selected a table in a corner. The
bartender, a squat, bald-headed man, wrapped in a huge
white apron, shuffled over to their table. He was
perspiring and Hastings was sure he detected a glimmer of
fear in the small man's eyes, as if the bartender could see
the friction in the air between the two newcomers.

"What'll it be, gents?" he asked in a cracked voice.

"Whiskey. Yer best," Johnson said. Then added, "and
two glasses."

"Are you drinking with both hands these days, Tuck?"
Hastings asked. "I'll have two beers," he said aside to the
bartender.

Johnson rocked back in his chair with a booming
laugh.

"Now, what do you know about that. I forgot you ain't
a whiskey-drinkin' man. One glass'll do, boy."

13

"Hell, Tuck, your memory ain't that short. Whiskey and guns don't mix I say."

"You always was an odd one, Bret-boy. Whiskey stirs up a man's blood, gives him an edge. Now, me, I can drink it like water. Dulls my senses a might if I drink enough of it, but I ain't yet been too drunk to yank this here hoglaig quicker'n any upstart who wants to test ole Tuck's reactions. Don't you forget that, Bret-boy!"

The bartender brought the drinks.

Hastings grasped one of the steins of beer and gulped it down, while Johnson drank from his tumbler like a man given water after a long, waterless struggle across a desert. His eyes didn't even tear. Hastings sipped the second beer slowly, trying to fathom Johnson's logic. That could prove difficult, for Johnson was seldom predictable. An idea dawned—a little something he had all but forgotten, but it might work and ease the present strained situation without spilling blood. It was worth a try.

"Tuck, I got here first. You claim that gives me no special rights since I ain't yet talked to Slater. I want to make this fair—give us both a square chance and the winner takes all. You interested?"

'What'll it be Bret-boy?' Johnson asked with a smile, his suspicion showing in his eyes.

"We cut cards," Hastings said. "High card talks to Slater."

"Fair enough," Johnson said, unable to pass up the challenge.

Hastings relaxed. The danger of an armed confrontation was past. A debt contracted was something he could count on Johnson to honor. Possibly this one sense of honor was the only decency in the man at all. Now even if he did lose, he was facing Johnson not with guns, but with cards. To Johnson the outcome, either way, was the same. Hastings would forfeit no pride.

Johnson dexterously fanned the cards out on the table,

selected one and turned it face up. A jack! Hastings studied the cards as if he could see through the backs of them. Finally, he reached out and flipped one over—the Queen of Hearts! An omen? Nonsense! He remembered the gypsy fortune teller in Wichita, then pushed the old woman out of his mind.

"Too bad, Tuck. Have a drink on me," he said, as he pushed back from the table and started toward the bar. Funny, he felt no elation over defeating Johnson at his own game—only a sense of release from an unwanted situation.

Hastings approached the bar. The click of his bootheels sounded hollowly in the empty room. The bartender, his back turned toward the pair, jumped noticeably as Bret approached. He turned, a grimace of fear etched on his face.

"You're might jumpy, friend. Where's Slater?"

"Ye...yes, sir. I didn't know but what you and your friend were Denton's men." The plump little man was still perspiring heavily. "Of course, you're not wearing the uniform, but..."

"Denton? What the hell you talkin' about, boy? Where's Slater?"

"He's in the back." The small man pointed a chubby finger toward the rear of the saloon. "Slater, that is."

"Thanks," Hastings said over his shoulder as he moved toward the indicated door. He didn't bother to knock. The man sitting at a desk looked up, a startled expression on his face. Hastings took a quick inventory of the office. It was typical of many saloon-keepers' quarters he was familiar with. A book shelf stood along one wall; a safe, a table, a worn leather couch with a chair to match, and a huge, scarred mahogany desk completed the furnishings.

"Who the hell are you?" the man asked, a tinge of anger in his voice.

Hastings ignored the question and took his time

15

studying the man. His neck was like a broom handle standing up from a pair of thin, bony shoulders, and a knob-like head topped it. His thick, dark hair was slicked down and a shade darker than his narrow eyebrows. As the man turned more towards him, Hastings could see that the right side of his face and a part of his hawkish nose were one massive bruise. A large splotch of purple, tinted green with edges of a sickly saffron color, seemed to be spreading over his cheek. The man gripped a quill pen between his long, slender fingers.

"Who are you?" The anger had been replaced by uncertainty.

"You Slater?" Hastings asked.

"Yes. Why? Did Denton send you?"

"Denton? No, nobody sent me. The name is Hastings. The word is out you need a gun. That right?"

"Well, maybe." He exhaled a sigh of relief. "Won't you sit down?" He indicated a leather chair with a talon-like finger. Hastings sat. Slater laid down his pen, then picked it up again. "How do I know you can handle a gun well enough to fill this position?" He had taken on an aura of confidence.

"I say I can! That's all you need to know. You want to hire a gun or not?" Anger had crept into his voice, and he edged forward. The confrontation with Johnson had frayed his nerves.

"Easy, Mr. Hastings." He was now talking like a man cajoling a small boy. "I see no reason why I should presume that you are the man I need. I am not at all sure you are capable of handling it." He extracted a large, black cigar from an inside pocket and busied himself with lighting it, still holding the pen between his fingers.

Hastings eyed Slater who was now rubbing his chin with the staff of the pen, the cigar clamped between two fingers at his side. He fought the anger bubbling within,

16

and with premonition, he slowly stood, crouched quickly, dropped his right hand, caught the gunbutt with three fingers, jerked upward, and forced the hammer back as his grip tightened on the butt. At the same time he squeezed the trigger with his index finger. The gun bucked in his hand, and the smell of cordite filled the air. The bullet snapped the staff of the pen, leaving Slater holding only a stub.

The whole action, from the crouch to the breaking of the pen, had occurred in the blinking of an eye.

Slater was stunned! His reaction was slow in coming, but when it did, it came almost in panic. He pushed back from his desk with enough force to slam his chair against the wall behind him, throwing his head back over the window sill hard enough to shatter the glass.

Hastings holstered his gun. It had been a damn foolish thing to do. Oh, it had impressed Slater all right, he could see that, but he could have killed him. It had been luck. Nonetheless, a gross distaste for Slater was rapidly growing within him.

Slater recovered quickly from his shock. He stuttered, "W...what the hell?"

Hastings smiled. Might as well push it for all it's worth, he thought. "You think maybe I can do the job?" he asked, sarcastically.

"Certainly, Mr. Hastings. The job is yours. With shooting ability like that, you are just what I've been looking for."

"About the job?" Hastings asked, his impatience growing.

"The job...yes. Ah...er...a...well, John Denton, he's crazy I tell you. Thinks he's a great soldier. Has his own army of sorts, even a fort." Slater was now spewing forth like a berserk Gatling gun. "He has two lieutenants: Burton, a quiet, ugly, little man; and Hardian, a brute. He did this." Slater pointed to his bruised and battered face. "I'll pay a thousand a head for those three and thirty a week while you wait."

Hastings missed the last about waiting. His revulsion mysteriously continued to grow. Funny, him looking down his nose at Frank Slater. Maybe he hadn't sunk as low as he thought he had. He leaned over the desk, resting his hands on the edge. His face was now inches from the bony, bruised face of the saloon keeper.

"You go to hell!" he spat. "I don't work for the likes of you for no amount of money."

"But wait a min..."

"Wait, hell! Not for you Slater. Maybe you're lucky though, because there's a gent out there as good as me with a gun who'll work for anybody who'll pay his fare. You proposition him, mister!" He stalked out of the door as Slater, mouth agape, sat at his desk unmoving.

Once outside the office, Hastings sighed as if some unclean thing had been washed away. "He's all yours, Tuck. I turned him down."

"Why? Somethin' wrong with the job? You turnin' yellow, Bret-boy?" He didn't mention the gunshot.

"Nope. Good pay and a reasonable request, I reckon. I found I have some principles after all. I can't take money from a man the likes of Slater. He's waitin' for you, Tuck. After my demonstration, he'll welcome you without question." He heard Johnson's hoarse laugh as he pushed out through the door.

2

Margaret Denton ambled along the boardwalk, clutching several small bundles in her arms. Shopping finished, she paused at the window of a tiny millinery shop to survey the latest fashions. The shiny glass caught her reflection. A stray wisp of ginger-colored hair strayed from the confines of her calico bonnet. She placed her packages along the narrow shelf below the window, freeing her hands to tuck the loose lock back beneath the bonnet's edge. She dawdled, studying her face framed by the broad arc of stiffly starched calico, delaying, as long as possible, her return to the carriage for the trip home.

The watchdog—as she called the tall, hard-muscled man assigned by her husband as a bodyguard—would be waiting. Each moment out of his sight was a cherished one for that was the only time she felt true freedom. The town's attitude toward her had changed since her marriage to John Denton—or was it she who had changed? Old friends avoided her now. She couldn't blame them. The whole town lived in fear—a fear that gnawed away at their very vitals. They all had been afraid of John, but no one would admit to it.

It was a latent spectre, hidden until that day she had stopped to talk to Arnold Patterson. When Beau Hardian had stepped between them and beaten Arnold with ruthless precision, the fear had become an open reality and they no longer strived to keep it hidden. Arnold had been a big man but, despite his size, he had been no match for the muscular Hardian. Beau had beaten him to death there in the street with his bare hands. Arnold, so slow he had not been able to land even one blow, was battered to a mass of bloody, pulpy flesh within a matter of minutes.

Other beatings had followed in the weeks and months that ensued. The victims were all strangers—unfortunate men, unwise enough to pay polite attention to her while whe was under the careful supervision of Beau Hardian. Even the giant of a prize fighter from back East had been no match for him. The pugilist had been hired by the boys in town to taunt Hardian into a fight. The big man had accepted the challenge, feeling over-paid for so light a task. Very confident of his prowess as a fighter, he had tried every insult imaginable to initiate a fight, but Hardian had ignored him as he might have ignored the nuisance of a barking dog. As a last resort someone had suggested he speak to Margaret Denton. As she had passed him on the boardwalk one day, he took her arm and attempted to talk to her. It was the last thing he ever did. Hardian hadn't let up his driving fists until the prize fighter had become the second man to die at his hands in Northgate. After this episode the town accepted its serfdom without resistance.

Margaret flipped her head back, aware that her mind had been wandering, and that the goods in the window were not holding her attention. She collected her bundles, blushing, and started toward the place she was to meet Hardian. She turned the corner and collided with a man going in the opposite direction. She felt herself falling, and her first reaction was to clutch the packages tightly to her breasts. Finally, her natural instincts caused her to throw out her arms behind her, dropping the bundles. As she hit the boardwalk with a hard thump, her legs splayed out before her. Her bonnet was knocked askew, and her hair fell loose around her shoulders.

The sharp pain she felt upon impact subsided and was replaced by a dull ache. Wiping away the tears, she saw before her a tall, lanky man dressed in faded dusty clothing with a large-holstered gun tied down to his leg. He was leaning over, mumbling apologies and trying with a clumsy effort to lift her to her feet. A shock of dark brown hair protruded from beneath a sweat-stained hat that had once been gray. His piercing blue eyes looked past a nose that was slightly crooked, probably broken in a fight many years ago. A stubble of beard and a drooping mustache, speckled with hairs of gray, decorated his face. A feeling of warmth radiated from him and enveloped her. She found herself liking this character with the lopsided grin spread across his face. He extended a hand and helped her to her feet, still mumbling apologies and grinning that ridiculous smirk which she found so very infectious. She wanted to laugh. The whole situation was so ludicrous—but then she remembered Beau. Fear clutched at her heart as she looked around frantically.

"Please, I can get those," she pleaded.

"Ma'am, I knocked them out of your arms. The least I can do is pick 'em up for you."

"Please," she said again desperately, "you don't understand. Just go, please. All you'll do is cause trouble."

He smiled as he handed her the last of the packages.

"Trouble?" He didn't finish his thought. Hardian stepped in, driving his massive fist into the stranger's unprotected face. The beating didn't last long, and Hardian stepped back from the stranger's body. Blood was oozing from several lacerations in the man's face, mingling with the dust of the street.

Margaret stood by, feeling helpless. Hopeless despair

21

filled her. The bitter taste of bile rose in her throat, and she swallowed hard, choking back the nausea which threatened to consume her. An urge to scream her anguish at the brute and to tear the flesh from his expressionless face swept through her. She fought against the impulse, knowing it would do no good. Beau was much stronger than she, and it would only complicate the situation when she had to face John. Anyway, it was too late to do anything for the man lying in the street. He was beyond her help now. Thus, when Beau grasped her arm in a painful grip, she returned meekly to the carriage. Beau pushed her up onto the seat with rough abandon, then leaped with nimble grace onto the seat beside her. She took a last look at the crumpled form of the man who had bumped into her. Her heart went out to him. She felt the hot sting of tears welling up in her eyes. As she dabbed at them with her handkerchief, she wondered whether he was dead or alive.

"Oh, no!" she sobbed as the carriage rolled away from the gathering crowd of curious onlookers. "Not another one! Oh, please, God, not another one!"

As they rolled along out of town and across the undulating prairie toward "Fort Denton", she shifted her attention to the man beside her. Beau was a very handsome man, she decided. She wondered why she had never really taken a good look at him before. Perhaps she had never consciously thought of him as a man, but only an instrument of her husband's psychotic intentions. She wondered how a man as beautiful as Beau could be so inhuman. She had never, on any occasion, observed him showing any emotional reaction, except for the momentary enjoyment of using his fists to pummel the life out of another man. Never in her presence had he ever lost his temper, nor was there ever any evidence of anger no matter what the circumstances. And Lord knows love and compassion were never traits to be shown. He undertook the beatings with the cool, methodical emotion of a machine—never with any fear. He seemed to be afraid of no one. Or was he? There was a shred of doubt in her mind. The unswerving loyalty to her husband, could that be based on fear? She cast the thought aside. Beau Hardian was capable of crushing John Denton to nothing with one hand. Yet there was no denying Hardian's loyalty. He was ready to do anything at any time for John Denton, but the reasoning behind this loyalty was a mystery. It certainly couldn't be money. He had accepted the responsibility of escorting her into town for John. At first she felt he was overdoing his task, but later she had come to realize that he was only doing her husband's bidding.

The carriage jolted to a halt along a quiet little stream with clear water trickling over a rocky bottom. Hardian jumped down and spread his bulk, belly down, on a slab of dark gray shale along the stream bank. He drank the cool water from cupped hands. Thirst satisfied, he plunged his head into the cool water, and brought it out sputtering like an old man and shaking his head like a shaggy dog trying to remove the excess water.

Margaret stepped down from the carriage, lifted her skirts high and joined Hardian on the rock slab which jutted out over the stream. She found by stretching out full length on her stomach and leaning over the edge that she could easily dip her hands into the cool, refreshing water. Following Hardian's example she used her hands as a cup. The water tasted sweet and moistened her parched throat. Much revived she sat up and made repairs on her disheveled hair. Through it all she took special pains to avoid any contact with Hardian, who was now standing over by the carriage, legs spread, hands on hips, gazing out over the rolling prairie. He was impatient to be

23

on his way, but he would say nothing about it, and she wondered if it would be futile to ask him the favor of saying nothing to John. She didn't like to beg, but John could be so cruel when he felt she had been indiscreet and Hardian would tell the story the way he saw it, or as he wanted to see it. Beau's reports to John were always exaggerated, sometimes only slightly and at other times grossly twisted. The first time she felt he was trying to punish her but, in time, she learned of other reports—reports in which she was in no way involved—which were not the whole truth. This one deviation was an enigma to her.

Margaret stood, smoothing her skirts as she walked over to Hardian and laid her hand gently on his forearm. Normally, he would have brushed it away. This time he ignored her and let her hand lie. Could she construe his lack of action as a concession?

"Beau, please don't tell John what happened!"

He looked at her as if she had asked him to betray his best friend, and screwing his face into a frown, he spat into the dust and said, "I'll tell what happened—that's all."

The rest of the ride was hot and uncomfortable. Dust wafted up from rolling wheels, saturating her hair and clothing and clinging to her face like a thin film of powder. Her mouth was dry and gritty. She held her handkerchief over her mouth, but the tiny cloth was too inadequate to be very effective. Despite the chilling fear of her coming confrontation with John which was slowly creeping over her as they neared the ranch, she wanted to be home. A cool drink of water to wash away the choking trail dust, a bath, and the cool secluded comfort of her room might be worth the agony she knew was coming. She tried to urge the horses to go faster. If anything, they only seemed to go that much slower.

24

Beau Hardian was oblivious to the heat, to the dust and to the dryness of the air. He sat upon his seat as if he were carved from granite and just as immobile. The only indication of life was a slow-spreading, dark stain of perspiration, seeping out from under his arms and fanning out across his back, and an occasional flick of the reins or a clucking noise to urge the horses on.

Beau brought the horses to a sliding halt in front of the wide veranda which traversed the front and two sides of the huge, rambling house. The impatient horses stamped and snorted, resenting the sudden halt. They craved water and the cooler comfort of the stable as much as their passengers sought relief from the heat.

Margaret slipped quickly to the ground and collected her packages. She glanced up at Hardian, a plea of hope poised on her lips, but he was looking straight ahead, dutifully awaiting her departure. Hurrying as quickly as her confining skirts would permit, she ran up the steps and into the cool, dim interior of the house, her final plea left unspoken. Once in her room, panting out of breath, she stored the things she had purchased that day and lifted the large porcelain pitcher and splashed some water into the matching bowl. The water was tepid, but it washed away the mixture of dust and perspiration, making her feel more relaxed and at ease. She poured water into an old china cup with a broken handle and gulped it down without stopping, then she lay back across her bed to await the arrival of her husband.

She heard a tapping on the door and roused herself up onto her elbows, aware that she had been dozing. A shiver of fear flashed through her breast, and she trudged to the door, patting her hair into place and straightening her skirts. John was just outside, standing at attention like a soldier awaiting an inspection; tall and erect, his shoulders thrown back and squared, a posture he always assumed. In their five years of marriage, she had never once seen him carry himself in any other way. And his clothes, like his posture, were perfect. The fit was just right—never too tight, never baggy, and always sharply creased and totally without wrinkles. The odd part was that she, as a wife, was never called upon to care for her husband's attire. He assumed the full responsibility for his appearance, and she had to admit that it was magnificent.

John pushed past her into the room, stride as precise as if measured and practiced. Margaret backed away and sat primly on the bed, her hands folded in her lap, her eyes fixed unmoving on a crack in the highly-polished, hardwood floor.

"Margaret!" Her name leaped at her. He was so slow to start, why couldn't he get it over with? Why did he have to drag it out? She glanced up at her husband standing in the center of the hooked rug—her mother's rug—legs spread, hands hidden behind his back. She looked at his face, and despair filled her. Her shoulders slumped and she wanted to hang her head, but that would only prolong the situation. The hopeless stage had been reached for he now wore his anger like a bright, red badge. His face was suffused with blood, imparting a dark crimson color to his skin, and his face was twisted into an expression of uncontrolable rage.

"Margaret!" he bellowed. "Why... tell me why you permit these strange men to be familiar with you right out in public view?" She could almost imagine smoke curling from his words. "If you persist in this outrageous behavior, I will have no alternative but to forbid you to go into town at all. Do I make myself clear?"

"John, I bumped into that man accidentally. He was only being kind in helping me to..." It was no use. He wasn't listening but had turned to stare out of the window.

"I'll have to have a talk with that marshal. What is his name?"

26

"Shane," she said. It meant nothing to him. He had shut her completely out of his conscious mind. His neck was a glowing pink, indicating a cooling of his emotions, and a small feeling of hope flitted through her heart.

"Shane. That's it—Ben Shane," he said to himself. "Damn ingrate! I brought him here to keep the streets free of riff-raff. I'll have Hardian convince him he needs to put a little more effort into his job, then everything will be just fine." He turned and glared at her. The memory of his purpose with her was flooding back.

Margaret watched the color seep into his face as his temper rose and fury enveloped him again. His head seemed to be transparent, and the red color rose rapidly up through his neck and face like the red fluid in a thermometer when held over a flame. She could imagine boiling, bubbling blood as the color climbed and she dreaded what was to come, but she knew there would be no reprieve.

Denton watched her. She couldn't identify the reasons behind his increasingly frequent tirades. He didn't seem at all like the suave, sophisticated man she had married, because then he had been so gentle, so loving. Most of the time now he was an inflamed, sadistic brute.

"Stand up, Margaret!" It was a command, lashed out in a gutteral tone like a top sergeant at the end of his patience with a raw recruit. She stood.

Denton glared at her from narrowed eyes with an icy glare of disgust, standing with no more than a foot separating them. With no warning and with amazing speed, he struck her with a backhand slap across her right cheek, and her head snapped to the left, her cheek stinging. His palm came back, fast, chafing her left cheek and snapping her head painfully to the right. She was amazed at the quickness of his movements for she had felt the smart of his blow before she was aware that he had even raised his hand. She fought the tears, but her eyes

27

filled and salty drops spilled out and raced down her throbbing, swollen cheeks.

John had not hesitated, but had followed the first blow with a series of the same. First, the backhand, then the palm, each time cracking her head back and forth until neck muscles ached with excruciating pain. At last he stopped, apparently finished for the time being.

Margaret found herself on her knees before him, weeping without control, and with no memory of sinking to her knees. Now, the realization that she was not capable of withstanding his punishment was the most humiliating of all. He turned and left the room without a word. As he closed the door, the latch clicked.

"Confined to quarters," she blubbered. Still sobbing profusely, she threw herself across her bed and let her emotions carry her away.

Sometime later, her eyes red and dry, her crying spell over, she rolled over onto her back and stared wide-eyed at the ceiling. She couldn't stand much more abuse, and there was no one she could turn to. Even her father could be no comfort now. Oh, if only she had listened to him, but he had been an old man and she was young and in love and had insisted she knew what she was doing. Could she convince the commandant at Camp Robinson that her husband was a threat to the whole territory? No, she would have to find her own way out of the mess which she had managed to place herself into.

3

Hastings awoke and gradually became aware of his unfamiliar surroundings. Nothing of the recent past was clear, and the room gave no hint of how or why he had come to be here. A large bed, piled high with comforters and feather beds, cradled his aching body. The room's single window, rimmed with fluffy, white curtains, drawn at the middle to either side, allowed sunlight to penetrate, limning dust motes floating lazily through the air.

A dull ache permeated his body. He lifted a heavy hand to his puffed, swollen face and jerked it away suddenly as he contacted a tender spot beneath his right eye. The pain jolted his brain, and some of the fuzziness washed away. Distorted memories of a severe beating, dust, an attractive girl, and a giant of a man came flooding back. There was no reasonable cause for the man's attack that he could perceive. Was it because he had bumped into the girl? Ridiculous! Yet she had been afraid of something. Had she known what was coming? There had to be a connection between her and the big man. The man was somehow responsible for her being in town, but what sort of relationship could exist between them? Husband and wife? No, surely not. She was such a pretty, sweet, fragile thing, and he such a violent roughneck of a man.

A tap-tap of clicking heels echoed down the hall, and the whisper of skirts sighed along the wooden floor. A young girl stepped into the room. She was smiling and her hair, the color of gold—no, more like ripe wheat—was twisted into braids, beribboned at the ends, forming tassels bound in scarlet, which hung down over her breasts. A white gown decorated with a multi-colored print was caught tight about her soft throat, clinched even more tightly at her narrow waist, and dropped away in flowing folds, swishing gently around her ankles and barely kissing the hardwood floor as she walked.

"Well, you're awake at last," she said, her face beaming with pleasure. He tried to sit up, but nausea turned his stomach, sending a retch of bitterness up into his throat. The room swam before his eyes, and pinpricks of pain dug deeply into the skin of his face. He slumped back into the pillows with a low moan.

"Be careful!" she said, concern creasing her face. She was beside the bed now, and he reached out, ignoring the pain, and took her hand in his. The hand was cool and soft.

"I reckon I ain't all together yet," he said. "I can't seem to move very well—not without a lot of pain and dizziness, anyhow. Who . . . who brought me here? Where am I? What happened? I reckon I really want to know what it was I did to get that big gent so riled with me."

"My, my," she said, laughing. "Beau sure didn't hurt your voice any. And your curiosity, Lord knows, is sure strong for a man so weak. You just sit back and rest, and I'll try to tell you all I know about it. Now, let me see . . . it was yesterday afternoon that Jed brought you here . . ."

"You mean I've been out all night! I can't believe it!"

"Please, sir, if you will quit interrupting me, I'll get on with it." She pulled the old rocker closer to the bed and sat down in it like a young mother preparing to tell her child a bedtime story. He could envision her beginning with the familiar "once upon a time". She was certainly not a mother but she was sure all woman—and about seventeen, he guessed.

The girl looked at him and smiled, rocked gently to and fro, appearing to be deep in thought as if the story had escaped her for the moment. She clasped her hands in her lap, enjoying the role she was playing to the utmost.

"It was just past noon when Jed brought you here. He was all excited about the fight. Said he had watched it all. Saw you bump into Mrs. Denton; saw Hardian hit you—the whole thing." She shrugged her shoulders. "Then Jed got a wagon from the livery, loaded you in and brought you here." She was so determined and so involved as she rocked, the sun glinting from her dark blonde hair.

"Jed said he figured Beau—the man who beat you—well, Jed thought Beau had made a big mistake, 'cause you're a gunfighter..." She paused, looking at him with a puzzled frown, "...not just one of the rowdies Beau usually fights with. Jed said you'd go gunning for Beau as soon as you're able." Her face twisted again into an enigmatic frown of uncertainty. "Would you? I mean, would you really shoot him? He doesn't carry a gun—ever!"

The question surprised him. Revenge hadn't occurred to him. There was no malice toward Hardian, no need for revenge was present. "No," he laughed, "I won't shoot the man. I suppose he was just doing what he thought necessary. But for the life of me, I don't know why."

"Daughter, is our guest awake?" a gruff, gravelly voice issued from the doorway.

"Yes, he is papa, and he'd be talking a streak if he wasn't so curious to know every little detail about what happened to him." She stopped rocking and turned in the

31

chair to look toward the portly old man who had just entered.

The old gentleman wore a blue, linen suit which was strained to cover his bulging middle. A white vest with pale-yellow stripes running through it, forming large checks, was decorated on one side by a gold watch, fob and chain, and his thick thumbs were hooked into the small pockets. A flowing, white beard and a magnificent handlebar mustache, waxed into precise, sharp tips, masked the lower part of a cherubic face. Eyebrows that were bushy rows of the same pale shade nearly covered limpid blue eyes.

"Fix the man something to eat, gal. The story-telling can wait. Now be quick about it." His voice had a rough yet gentle quality about it.

"Yes, Papa." The girl rose quickly and left the room.

The old man seated himself in the chair she had vacated, found a long, thin cigar in his inside jacket pocket, bit off the end, tongued it from end to end, clamped it tightly between strong teeth, and lit it. "My name is Colonel Tatum P. Graham," he said. "That title is a holdover from the era of the great war of the Confederacy, but I like it, and that's what most people call me—Colonel that is. Of course, I was never in the army. How do we call you, son?" The request was polite and unassuming but still gruff.

"Bret Hastings," he said, feeling like a prisoner undergoing interrogation, but then he relaxed, for he was certain he had detected a warm, friendly smile beneath the bushy, white whiskers.

The old man blew a thin stream of blue-white smoke ceilingward. "You tangled with one of Denton's men, son. Now, it won't go any further unless you push the issue, and I wouldn't advise that. I'm not saying I wouldn't like to see someone push Denton, but it's not a healthy thing to do."

32

Was the old man putting a challenge to him—coaxing him into declaring himself about Denton? Trouble was not what he needed. He had enough of that without taking on a man he didn't even know. "Who is Denton?" he asked. "It seems everyone I've talked to—well, anyway, Frank Slater and you have mentioned him."

"You mixed with Slater, son? It's none of my business, but Slater is no good. I don't like him and I don't trust him. In some ways he's worse than Denton." Disappointed concern filled the old man's voice and a sudden chill seemed to fill the room. Hastings felt as if his welcome had suddenly been worn out. He told the old man about his encounter with Slater, and as he finished the story, the old man's features softened.

"A wise choice, son. Slater is a bad one. So is Denton, but he's twice the man Slater will ever be. Nevertheless, I never saw any good in Denton. Most hereabouts thought a lot of him at first, but he changed just like I sensed he would."

Just then the girl came back, flowing into the room, balancing a tray bearing a bowl of steaming broth and a tall, foam-capped glass of milk.

Hastings salivated at the sight of food, realizing just how hungry he was.

"Well, daughter, do you think our guest can manage that for himself?"

"Oh, I'm sure he can, Papa," she replied. "You can, can't you?" she asked Hastings.

"Excuse me son, I'm not much of a host. This is my daughter, Laural."

She set the tray across his lap and fluffed up the pillows behind him. Hastings smiled at her as he clumsily lifted a spoon of hot, savory broth to his mouth.

She smiled back and said, "Well, I'll leave you two alone. I'm sure Papa is anxious to tell you a lot of stories. He just loves to talk." She winked at Hastings and left the

33

room, jubilant and humming softly to herself.

The old man reddened slightly and puffed on his cigar as Hastings spooned thick, tasty soup into his mouth.

"Let's see...it was about six years ago that Denton arrived here in Northgate. A dandy all right, dressed in expensive clothes like a dude fresh out of the East. Funny—that's just what he was then. To the ladies, though, he was a real dashing character and had plenty of money. I guess the young ladies of Northgate considered him a prize catch. Thank God, Laurie wasn't old enough for marriage! I suspect there were a number of young girls who set their caps for him, and he courted them all one by one, like he had to give them all a chance. I'm sure he stole the heart of more than one. He was like a buyer picking and choosing the goods he wanted to buy, and he had his pick, don't doubt that for a minute! Margaret Taylor finally won out...or is it lost out? Oh, well, they were married. Believe me there were some mighty unhappy young ladies around here for a time....Say, you want more soup?"

"No, no that was fine. Maybe a little more after a while."

The old man took the tray and set it on a table at the far end of the room. Returning to his seat in the rocking chair, he fished another cigar out of his inside pocket and lit it.

Hastings wore a pensive look. "Seems to me you're tellin' me about two different people," he said.

The old man rolled his smoking cigar between a pudgy thumb and forefinger. "Now, hold on, Mr. Hastings, I was just getting to the other part." The Colonel knocked ash from his cigar. "Not long after he and Miss Taylor returned from honeymooning in San Francisco, the change began. It had something to do with Hardian's arrival, although Denton dominates Hardian completely...for some unknown reason.

34

Hastings shifted his position and grimaced with pain.

The old man continued. "Hardian rode into town one day and asked where he could find John Denton. The next time we saw them they were dressed in those flashy, brown uniforms."

The sound of a galloping horse echoed in the distance. The Colonel turned toward the window and listened intently. Hastings followed the old man's example and turned his attention toward the sound of the horse which was drawing near.

"That fellow, whomever he is, is sure pushin' that hoss," Hastings said.

"He is at that," the Colonel agreed, a puzzled frown crossing his brow. "There's no reason for anyone to be racing out here. Laurie and I don't have much to do with townspeople." The Colonel was quite perturbed about the horseman. Is it because I'm here? Hastings pondered. He tried to rouse himself, but the effort made the room spin and the pain became unbearable. He fell back among the bed clothes, a cold sweat covering him.

The sound of horse's hooves pounding against the ground ceased. The rider was here!

The Colonel sat immobile in the rocking chair. His teeth clamped tightly around his cigar. Hastings could see the violent action of his jaw muscles. Withered hands clutched the rounded arms of the chair, his knuckles white with the pressure exerted by his grasp.

The girl! My God! The girl! Where is she? I've got to do something, Hastings thought. He tried to swing his feet over the side of the bed and to lift his head, but the effort was too much for him and he fell back to the pillow. The world sped away from him, pulling behind it a cloud of black-black smoke shutting out all the light.

Hastings awoke a few moments later. The Colonel was still sitting in his chair. Laurie, her cool hand on his forehead—the other hand holding his wrist, counting his pulse—was also in the room and safe. Another old man was standing next to the Colonel's chair. Hastings recognized him as the old fellow from the hotel porch.

"Howdy, young feller," the newcomer greeted him. His words were slurred, and toothless gums were visible through his bushy whiskers. A black beard contrasted strikingly with the fringe of slate-gray hair around his head above his ears and the bald pate above them.

"This is Jed Bannock, the one who brought you here," Laurie said.

"Jed, the old rascal, like to have scared me to death bolting out here the way he did. It's not like me to get bothered over a lone horseman, but I didn't know who it could be. Just didn't figure on Jed," the Colonel said with obvious embarrassment. "What was the rush for anyway, Jed?"

"Nick Burton was in town tuhday. Now, he don't come tuh town 'less'n he's ahuntin' trouble. He nosed around some, had a drink er two but stayed clear of Slater's."

"Who's Burton?" Hastings asked.

"Burton is another of Denton's lieutenants," the Colonel said." He came to town just after Hardian —maybe two weeks later. He's a skinny, bandy-legged little runt. They say no one is faster with a gun than he is, though."

Jed interrupted, "It was right after he got here that Denton's Army begin tuh grow. He sure recruited quick, picked up drifters, saddle tramps, and anyone'd work fer what he pays. Wages is purty good, as I hear it."

The Colonel said, "Yes, it was about that time that our town marshal was shot, and before we knew it, Ben Shane was toting a badge. It was then that the town folks began to realize that John Denton owned them. There wasn't any of them brave enough to do anything about it. He doesn't bother this town much but he makes it clear he

36

controls it and woe be to the man who goes against him!"

Jed spoke up. "It ain't really been so bad, long as yuh live the way he wants. Now, me, I'm too lazy tuh resist." Jed twisted the ends of his mustache as he spoke. "Hey, just thought yuh might want tuh know 'bout Burton nosin' around. Anyhow, it gives me a' excuse tuh get some of Laurie's good vittles."

"I might have known you had an ulterior motive, you old scalawag. But why did you run that horse for?" the Colonel asked.

"I jist run him the last quarter mile tuh see iffen I could still sit a saddle," Jed said.

Laurie had slipped unnoticed from the room while the men talked. She returned now as the two old friends continued to exchange pleasantries.

"If you two can stop yarning long enough to eat, dinner is ready," Laurie said.

Hastings noticed she carried his tray. This time it bore more solid food, and he was anxious to dig in. She set the tray before him, smiled, and followed her father and Jed from the room.

4

The days dragged as Hastings mended. The lacerations healed, and the large, purple bruises faded until only patches of saffron-yellow skin remained. Weakness was turning to strength, but the pain lingered on. Several weeks had passed since Jed had brought him here, but how many, he wasn't sure.

He had not fully recovered, but he was strong enough to saddle and ride. The thought of leaving caused some misgivings. These three people had aided him during a trying time. They had made a home for him. Since old Mose had died, they were the first to show they cared. His plans had called for an early start today, but Laurie had convinced him he should wait and say goodbye to Jed who was expected for a visit later in the day. He acquiesced, knowing he was in the old man's debt.

Jed, as was his custom, arrived in sufficient time to partake of the noon meal. He was his excited old self with many tall tales to relate.

At long last they seated themselves around the table for a farewell meal. Hastings caught himself bolting his food as if the end of the meal would relieve the tenseness of the situation and make it easier for him to leave. He should be savoring the food for it would be the last homecooked meal he would have for a long time. His impatience was, in part, due to his reluctance to bid farewell to these people who had befriended him. They had asked nothing of him, but had come to his assistance when he had needed it most. They were friends—friends like he had never known before. Now, he must leave because his past wouldn't let him rest. Anxiety arose from his disappointment at not finding the man for whom he searched, and he ached to be on his way to continue his endless search. The man had to be found before he could rest, but beyond that, he could imagine nothing. He had never pictured himself as the loser in the encounter; but even if he did win, with a past so filled with lust for revenge, what could the future possibly hold? Now, for the first time since he had left Georgia, he had found a place where he felt he belonged.

Hastings led his big black horse around to the front of the house. He shook Jed's gnarled old fist. There was plenty of strength left in the old man's grip. The Colonel's hand was soft and pudgy and exerted very little pressure against his own. Laurie looked up at him, tears ready to brim over in her eyes. She moved closer, stood on tiptoe, slipped her arms around his neck, pulled his head lower and kissed him full on the lips. An urge to crush her against him, hug her tightly and return the kiss with all the fever he felt burning inside him rose, but he resisted the impulse and instead stepped into the saddle.

Forcing himself not to look back, he left the Graham's and headed south, following the river valley. The trail was only faint in places and little used in recent years. He chose the path along the river to avoid the town—a choice of habit, but he found himself frequently avoiding clusters of people unless he had business with them, and his business in Northgate was finished.

Riding along the stream was comfortable and pleasant.

A slight breeze stirred among the branches of the cottonwood trees which grew profusely along the bank, sometimes all but obscuring the trail. Birds chirped merrily but otherwise there was a luxurious stillness to the world. Heavily wooded areas were interspersed here and there with clearings. While crossing one of these open areas, he became aware of the ominous, dark clouds spreading across the southwestern sky. The thought of a storm disrupting the peacefulness of his quiet day was discomforting, especially with no more shelter provided than the trees could afford.

He rode out of the clearing, through another wooded area, and up onto a grassy knoll which was slightly higher than the general level of the stream bank. From this vantage point he saw the shack. It was constructed mostly of clapboards with a makeshift porch and was backed up against a ridge which rose a hundred feet above the stream level on the shore opposite his position. A door was on the front side of the near corner with two windows. A lazy column of smoke drifted upward along the face of the bluff. A weed-infested garden, enclosed by a crude rail fence, occupied a portion of the area in front. Farther along the bluff, north from the shack, was a tumbled-down barn of the same roughhewn wood as the house. Along one side was a battered old buckboard with one wheel missing. An aged, worn harness hung from a peg on a door which was slightly ajar.

The shelter would provide adequate protection from the storm. He spurred his horse along the bank until he found a shallow ford and splashed across the stream. He reached the shed just as the first large drops of rain splattered against the roof. Inside, he found an aging mule contentedly munching hay in one of the stalls. The second stall was vacant. He unsaddled his horse, rubbed him down and gave him a portion of grain found in a bin on the opposite wall.

The rain was heavy and ominous. Making sure the shed door was closed, he made a dash for the porch on the old shack. The thirty yards were crossed without getting more than a superficial wetting. As he raised his left hand to knock, his right hand dropped to the butt of his gun, lifted it gently out of the holster and eased it back into place. His knock was answered promptly by a shaky old voice inviting him to enter.

The inside of the house reflected the conditions of the outside. The floor was of hard-packed earth. The walls were unadorned and, in places, the waning daylight was showing through various-sized cracks. A rickety old table, grayed with age, occupied the center of the room. A dilapidated cot covered with threadbare blankets reposed along one wall. A stove, constructed of stones cemented together with clay, covered with a blackened iron grate, supported a skillet, a large kettle, and a coffee pot, all of which were as soot-covered as the grate on which they rested. Bending over the stove in a permanent, stooped position was a shaggyhaired old man. His back was to Hastings, his hands busy with something frying in a skillet. He wore no shirt. His spare, stooped shoulders were covered only with faded red longjohns and galluses which supported his worn, baggy britches. He remained stooped as he turned, clutching the skillet handle. The savory odor of frying bacon filled the room. A pleasant face which may have borne a smile met Hastings' eye, but he couldn't be sure since the entire face was hidden by a bushy beard and eyebrows equally as unkempt as the mop of hair which fell shoulder length about his face.

"Howdy," Hastings said. "That grub sure smells good."

41

"Howdy, stranger. Sit a might. There's plenty o' grub here for the both of us," he said in the same shaky voice. "Bad night to be ridin'. If ye ain't in no hurry, ye might stay a spell. I don't see many folks out this way. Sit, and I'll finish up this here grub."

Hastings sat on a chair that looked to be in danger of collapse. His back was to the door and the front window which made him feel somewhat ill-at-ease but it was the position indicated for him and, after all, he was an uninvited guest.

"Ye headin' south or air ye jist goin' into Northgate?" the old man asked.

"South," Hastings said, not willing to commit himself too far.

"Been in Northgate long?"

"Long enough. Too long to suit my likings. I was there a bit more'n a month.

"Was a nice place once. I was one o' the first settlers here abouts. Lived in town until Denton moved in. After he took my daughter, I didn't see no need to stay and truck with that sneaky no-account, so I moved out here along the river and commenced to farmin'. Ain't had no truck with him since." He looked inquiringly at Hastings. "How's come ye air a ridin' the river bank anyhow? Folks jist don't come this-a-way much anymore."

"It's a mite cooler among the trees than it is out on the main trail," Hastings said noncommitally.

"That it is, that it is," the old man said. He forked several thick, crisp slices of bacon onto two chipped plates, ladled a generous helping of steaming beans along beside the bacon and placed the plates on the table, together with two mugs of hot, black coffee. Then he motioned for Hastings to eat.

Hastings stuffed his mouth alternately with large helpings of bacon and beans, washing them down with scalding, bitter coffee. The old man was doing justice to his food, gripping his fork like a skinning knife and eating as if his life depended on his finishing before his guest.

Outside, night had fallen, enveloping the abode in a shroud of black. The storm seemed to have reached a peak, as rain slashed down and was whipped with frenzy against the walls and windows of the house. The two men seated at the table ignored the rolling thunder, the wind-whipped rain and howling wind. Hastings was intent only on devouring the food before him and enjoying the soothing warmth of the fire smouldering in the stone stove. The old man seemed to be talked out for the time being.

The crack of a rifle, followed instantly by a tinkle of breaking glass, raised the hackles along Hastings' neck and sent shivers down his arms. A whistle of air rushed past his ear. The old man toppled over as if blown backwards by the force of a large explosion. Hastings grabbed the lamp with his left hand and chopped at the chimney with his right, shattering the glass and extinguishing the light. Throwing himself to the floor, he rolled away from the table and lay motionless for a moment, letting his eyes adjust to the dark. Slowly, he got to his feet and edged silently through the dark interior of the cabin to the door. His hand found the latch and lifted it. Coolness pervaded his body. There was no fear now, only a calm, dogged determinism. He was a man without a nerve in his body.

Jerking open the door and palming his six-gun, he lunged into the inky blackness. A flash of lightning outlined briefly a black, shadowy figure rising out of the mud, gun in hand. His gun bucked in his hand. Once! Twice! Had he been shooting only at an image impressed on his vision by the brief flash of light? Had he hit his adversary? Doubt rammed through him, and a cold sweat drenched him. He dodged off the porch into the noisy blackness of the night and the chill of slashing rain.

Another bolt rent the darkness. Nothing moved. Hastings sloshed his way toward the place where he had last seen the shadow. His foot struck an obstacle, and he leaned over, straining his eyes. A body lay face down in the mud. He reached out and grabbed the soaked coat collar of a man. Then he dragged the body to the limited protection of the porch.

He re-entered the shack, leaving the mud-splattered body of the nocturnal intruder in the sparse protection of the porch. The old man lay where he had fallen, splintered pieces of chair scattered about his inert form. Hastings moved closer, knelt and placed an ear against the rough, woolen fabric covering his chest. He rose slowly. The old man was dead, but he meant nothing to Hastings. He'd known him such a short time. There was no remorse, no sense of loss, no anger, only the cool-calm nonfeeling of a man without emotions. The gaping wound at the juncture of the old man's throat and torso had ceased welling blood.

Outside, the wind drilled into him making walking difficult, and the rain bit spitefully into his face. Grasping the dead man's coat collar, he dragged him inside, kicking the door closed with a bootheel. Stripping two of the worn, threadbare blankets from the bed, he covered the bodies.

With the unpleasant task completed, he stripped off his own wet clothing, arranging it around the stone stove, dried his gun carefully, took a can of oil from a shelf and oiled the gun well. Finally, he rolled up in the one remaining tattered blanket, stretched out on the old cot and was instantly asleep.

Morning dawned with sun glaring through curtainless windows, and lighting the interior of the shack. Hastings dressed quickly but took time to oil the inside of the stiff, dry holster, rubbing the oil well into the leather with an old rag. He buckled on the cartridge belt, tied the rawhide thongs around his thigh and slid the gun into the oiled holster. He drew—whipping the gun out of the holster with a practised ease. Satisfied, he set about preparing breakfast.

Outside, evidence of the storm had all but vanished. The only indication of the violent rain was a few widely dispersed puddles of mud already drying in the heat of the morning sun. A large branch had been partly broken from the tree, reinforcing his guess that the assassin had crouched on the tree limb while making the shot which had killed the old man.

Hastings saddled his black and put a halter on the mule. One by one he dragged the dead men out and lashed them securely, side by side, across the mule's back.

As he turned from the mule toward his horse, his eye caught the flashing glimmer of the sun reflected from a partially-covered shiny object in the drying mud. Stepping across the short distance, he retrieved the object. He wiped away the crusted earth to reveal a fancy rifle. It was a Sharp's .50 calibre buffalo rifle. The metal parts had been nickel-plated and engraved with fancy scroll work. The stock was carved with intricate scrolls as well, encompassing two letters carved in old English script. The letters were the initials: T.J. Stuffing the rifle into his saddle boot, he mounted the black, grabbed the rein for the mule and rode out at a distance-consuming lope toward town. A look of profound determination creased his face.

Things weren't the way they should be. It's Tuck's rifle right enough. But why did he want that ole man killed for? Hell! It wasn't the old man that Jasper was after—it was me, Hastings thought. His life was owed to a sudden gust

45

of wind or splash of rain in the eyes of the rifle holder. No doubt about it. Still it wasn't like Tuck to send someone to do his killin' for him. No, Tuck would do that himself. Then how does one explain the killer? Yet, there was no denying the rifle was Johnson's, and Tuck prized it very highly even though he seldom used it. He'd won it in a shooting match years ago, and it had remained his favorite possession. No, he wouldn't loan it, and there just isn't any way a body could get it without Tuck knowing about it. Hastings scratched his head and urged the black into a faster pace.

The marshal's office was located at the north end of River Street. Hastings secured his mount and the loaded mule to the hitching rail and entered the office. A deputy was tilted back in a swivel chair, his feet propped up on a scarred, rolltop desk. His arms dangled over the sides of the chair, barely brushing the floor. He snored loudly.

Hastings, smiling, gently shook the man awake.

"Who...who...what the hell is goin' on here?" he sputtered, coming awake very slowly. The chair hit the floor with a dull thud, forcing his booted feet to smash painfully to the floor.

Hastings stepped back, grinning. "Hold on, Sheriff, I got a couple of dead folks you might want to take a look at. Seems they got themselves shot up some."

"I ain't no damn sheriff! I'm a deputy town marshal," he said, his voice rising as if the mistake was of worldshattering importance. Belatedly, he said, "Dead men! Damn! Whur are they? Who are they? What happened?" He was dancing around not sure of what he should do. His gunbelt, buckled too loose for his bony hips, kept sliding down and interfering with his attempts at walking. He followed Hastings outside, forgetting his hat and tugging at the sagging gunbelt. The sun struck his bald dome, making it shine like raw gold.

46

Hastings found it difficult to confine his laughter at the ludicrous image of the deputy prancing toward the load-burdened mule, clutching desperately at the gunbelt. The man's excitement at suddenly being cast in an important role increased the humor of the moment. He was obviously impressed with himself as a deputy. He approached the mule cautiously as if the bodies might rise up at any moment and attack him, and very carefully he lifted the corner of the blanket.

"Why that's Ike Henry!" he exclaimed. "He's the swamper over at Slater's Saloon. Works for room and board and drinks—drinks mostly." He glanced quickly under the other blanket, carefully avoiding contact with the dead body.

"Holy hell! That's old man Taylor! There's gonna be hell to pay for that." He seemed unaware that he was talking of the men as if they were still alive. He turned to look at Hastings, his face pale, his eyes twitching nervously as if he were the one responsible for the deaths. "How'd it happen?"

Hastings related the story, not embellishing it any or mentioning Tucker Johnson's fancy rifle.

The deputy shook his head slowly in disbelief. "Yuh say Henry shot Taylor and you shot Henry?"

"That's the way it happened," Hastings said, somewhat annoyed.

"Wal, I reckon there's no need to hold yuh. Denton's gonna be mad as a rag-tailed dog when he finds out. Taylor was his wife's old man yuh know."

"No, I didn't know," Hastings said.

"Whur yuh headed, now? Yuh stayin' in town?"

"Nope. I'm riding on south, probably to Kansas City where I was going in the first place."

He mounted his horse and turned him south along River Street, leaving the deputy standing beside the mule

47

and its burden. He swung west at the Town's main intersection and rode down to Slater's Saloon and dismounted with the intention of going inside to confront Johnson. He didn't quite make it. Johnson met him at the door.

"You goin' somewhere, Bret-boy?"

"Just brought your rifle back, Tuck. You're gettin' a might careless with it these days."

"That's my rifle sure enough. Where did you come by it?"

Hastings sensed something in the air that was not quite right. He dropped his right hand lower and closer to the handle of his Colt. Johnson seemed wary, sort of bristling like a trapped peccary.

"Fella took a shot at me and missed last night. Now, how do you suppose that Slater's drunk got a hold of Tucker Johnson's prized shooting piece long enough to try and put an end to me?"

"Sorry about that, Bret-boy, but I hadn't missed it yet. I reckon Henry could have swiped it without me knowin'. I just don't pay much attention to the likes of him nohow."

Hastings wasn't convinced and suspicion curled around his mind. "Now, I find that mighty interesting. How did you know I meant Henry? I didn't mention any names."

Johnson grinned broadly. "You said Slater's drunk, Bret-boy. There just ain't nobody else fits that name like Ike Henry did."

Hastings was stumped. Ike Henry didn't take it upon himself to try and kill him. Someone had to have put him up to it. But who? "You let the likes of Henry borrow your fancy rifle these days, Tuck?"

"I didn't say I loaned it, Bret-boy, but that ain't sayin' he couldn't have got in and took the rifle with me not

48

knowin' about it. Them cards keep me pretty busy, along with the body guardin'."

He seemed to be apologizing which increased Hastings' alertness because that wasn't at all like the Tucker Johnson he thought he knew so well.

"I'd buy you a drink, Bret-boy, but Slater, he says you ain't welcome here no more. You know what he told me?" Johnson stepped closer carrying out his little act as if he had a highly secret message to deliver. Hastings relaxed, his entire being felt loose, and his right hand was poised and ready.

Johnson looked both ways and then spoke in a hoarse whisper. "Slater said I was to shoot you on sight if you should come near here again. He put a price on your head—a right good one at that. Now, you know me, Bret-boy, I have a hankerin' to collect that money, but I figure I owe you a favor. I'm in debt to you for this job. Don't that beat all?" He stepped back, all signs of his little game gone. Hastings realized that despite his threatrics, Johnson was dead serious.

"Now, Bret-boy, you climb up on that black hoss and you ride, because next time I see you, I'll come a shootin'."

Hastings shrugged his shoulders. He had no quarrel with Johnson. Tuck meant what he said. There probably was a good price on his head. The one thing he couldn't figure was why Tuck didn't try to collect it now. It was hard to believe that Tucker Johnson had turned down the prize because of any compassionate feelings towards him or because of any feelings of indebtedness the job might have incurred.

He turned and descended the steps, shaking his head in disbelief. A steady clump of bootheels sounded along the boardwalk, and a loud voice rasped out at him, loud and ringing with authority.

"Wait up, Hastings!"

Hastings spun full around and stepped into the street, alert and ready, crouched with his right foot slightly ahead of the left.

The owner of the voice was a tall, broad-shouldered man who was striding toward him with his obsidian-black hair flying in the breeze unconfined by a hat. His skin was a dark brown, and at first he took him to be an Indian. The flashing star pinned high on his suede vest told him that this was Ben Shane. Except for the barehead, and clean-shaven face, he looked the part of a town marshal. He carried his gun tied low on his left side. His long right arm swung free, but his left was stiff and bent at the elbow. Hastings relaxed and stood straight.

"I want a few words with you, gunman. You'd best be able to explain those two bodies you so handily delivered to my doorstep!" Shane apparently was used to giving orders and having them instantly obeyed.

"Well, now, Mr. Shane, I told the whole story to your deputy. So why don't you ask him for the details?"

"Don't play smart with me, gunman. I did just that. Now, I want you to tell me about it and leave out the sarcasm, you hear?" The commanding tone still existed, and Shane looked confident and very much at ease like he was merely passing the time of day.

Hastings tensed, then shrugged off the tension as he hunched his shoulders. The last thing he wanted was to precipitate gun play. He was anxious to leave, and a shoot out with Shane would gain him nothing. So, he very patiently related for the second time the events of the previous night. At the end of his exposition he paused, looking Shane directly in the eyes, indicating that as far as he was concerned, the subject was closed.

Shane glanced down and commenced to describe little circles in the dust with his boot toe. At last he looked up at Hastings and spoke. "Hastings, I have no reason to doubt you. Something tells me I'm making a mistake letting you go, but you listen and you listen well. You get out of this town and you stay a long way away from here for as long as I wear this badge. Next time I see you, I'll throw your ass in jail 'till it rots, and if you should try to resist, I'll shoot and I'll shoot to kill. So, heed my warning and get out now!" The now was emphatically clear. Shane was a man to be wary of.

Hastings, somewhat subdued, stepped into the saddle, tipped his hat to the marshal, and headed his horse toward the street. He had never stood and taken a tongue lashing like that one and he felt cowed, but his desire to leave dominated his emotions.

Just then, from the far west end of town, a buggy, tearing through the rutted street, spewing out a great cloud of dust, hurtled past him, causing his horse to rear. Although his view of the man and the woman huddled within the carriage was only momentary, he recognized the ginger-haired young lady. His encounter with her had led to his severe beating at the hands of her husband's lackey not far from this spot. But it wasn't Margaret Denton that attracted most of his attention. For Hastings recognized the man beside her as the man he had sought all these many years. He did not know that that man and John Denton were one and the same! He muttered a string of curses and viciously spurred his horse in pursuit of the racing buggy.

5

The racing horse carried Hastings across River street, past the line of buildings which formed a shadowy fort against the stream bank, and over the broad ledge of shale which provided a fetlock-deep ford across the sluggish stream. Once across Hastings urged the tiring horse up the long, gentle incline. After a mile of hard riding, he brought his lathered steed to a halt. They rested atop a long ridge overlooking the town. Hastings could see a troop of brown-clad soldiers, still mounted, and fanned out in an orderly, semicircular line facing the marshal's office.

The last minute decision not to confront Denton had been a wise choice. Most surely the soldiers would have shot him had he, in his fit of anger, killed their leader. The situation had not lessened his hatred for the man. The rage was real, and the desire to inflict as much pain as possible was still his one driving force. No, his reason for sparing the man was a much greater one than death. Killing Denton now would be too easy. His death had to be a slow, painful ordeal. Denton had to suffer as he had suffered so long ago and he had to pay for all the suffering since then. Denton must know who was hunting him; to know his time was near; to fear a death which could strike at any moment, and to know that he, Hastings, was choosing the time. This was the only way he could avenge the pain of his tragedy.

Two tiny figures perched on the boardwalk, like minute dolls, gestured at one another. Even from this distance he had no trouble identifying them as John Denton and Ben Shane. They seemed to be arguing, and Denton was doing most of the talking if his excessive arm movements were any indication. Shane and Denton finished their discussion. A detail of four men broke off from the troop and galloped north, and the Dentons and Shane disappeared inside the marshal's office.

With Denton out of view, he turned his thoughts to his immediate future. Leaving Northgate was out of the question as long as Denton lived. Yet, he couldn't return to the town itself, not unless he wanted to face a confrontation with both Shane and Johnson. A smile crossed his face. He nudged his horse into a slow walk and headed in an easterly direction. The sun was over his right shoulder. At this slow pace, it would take him an hour or so, and he would be a bit early for supper.

The place looked deserted as he approached through the gate, slid gently to the ground, and secured his horse. Quiet hung in the air, and a cloud of gloom encompassed him as he walked lightly across the oak-floored porch. He tapped softly on the wooden door. After a short interval, he rapped again. This time, muffled footsteps approached the door. It swung wide and there stood Laurie wearing a frock of some soft, green material. Laurie, an image of beauty, her velvet loveliness creating an ache in his heart. Dainty pink hands set off the snowy lace of dress cuffs, and lustrous gold hair twined over and around the lacy dress collar. The power of her beauty brought a smile to his face and an aching to his loins. The finest silks and satins couldn't have made her any more fetching to him

53

than she was at that moment with the lime-green enhancing her golden and somewhat disheveled hair. I've been too long without a woman, he thought.

"Bret. Oh, Bret! You've come back," she cried as she rushed into his arms.

Hastings, taken aback by her aggressive action, found himself kissing her as he held her tightly in his arms, savoring her nearness. He tasted the sweet flavor of her lips which seared his with the intensity of a burning fever. Bewildered, he wasn't at all sure just what he should do and, as a result of his confusion, he did nothing except withhold his pent-up emotions. It was Laurie who finally broke away with a long, shuddering sigh and gazed up into his eyes with a tender longing.

"Laurie . . ."

The proper words he needed to express his thoughts were elusive. How could he tell her they shouldn't do this—shouldn't permit their emotions to carry them away like this. How did he explain that he was not worthy of her love, that he was a man more dead than alive who had but a single purpose in life and when that was accomplished. . . . Love for a woman was a feeling completely foreign to him. During his wanderings he had not had time for women, except for the kind that inhabited the many saloons he frequented. They served a need but they never really seemed like women—not the kind of woman a man could love. The decent women were out of his reach. The fact that he divided women into two groups, the good and the bad with no in-between, never occurred to him as anything unusual. Laurie was one of the "good" and, therefore, he had no right to her except at a discreet distance. Moreover, she was so young. The feelings he had for her, could they be love or was it simply desire? A desire he had not permitted himself to feel for a decent girl before.

"Papa is napping," she said. "Come on in but try to be quiet. The old dear was just exhausted today. I think he found your leaving very trying. I know I did. He's very fond of you, you know. I do believe he looks upon you as the son he never had." She led him into the kitchen, stoked the fire in the old wood stove, and put the coffee pot on to heat.

"Why did you come back, Bret? We were so sure we would never see you again and here you are! I guess it really doesn't matter. I'm just happy that you're back. You will stay this time won't you? Papa will be so glad to see you again—Jed too."

They seated themselves at the cloth-covered table, and Laurie gazed cow-eyed at him. He shifted uneasily in his chair trying to find a comfortable position. She had a perpetual little smile, with only the corners of her pouted lips turned up, which disarmed him. She rested her chin in her hands while she studied him. A conscious feeling of discomfort plagued him, and his emotions tugged him in opposite directions. He pondered her questions for a moment, trying hard not to look her directly in the eyes. In relating the incidents of the morning and the night before, he was careful to avoid any mention of John Denton.

Just as he finished telling Laurie, the Colonel shuffled into the kitchen. He breathed a sigh of relief and felt much more at ease now that he was no longer alone with the girl.

"Howdy, Bret," the Colonel drawled, "I thought I heard your voice. Damn! I'm right glad to see you back. Whatever it is that brought you to us again, I'm happy for it. This time you are going to stay and that's final. How about some coffee, daughter, or are you trying to boil it all away just to moisten up this infernal dry air?"

Hastings retold once more the events that had transpired since he had left. As the afternoon passed into evening, he told and retold the story or, at least, parts of it several times. He thought of the scavengers who haunted saloons, always ready and willing to listen to tales spun by those who drifted from place to place, tales which gave these scavengers a vicarious thrill and brought some adventure into their stolid lives. They were not only willing to listen but encouraged the telling and retelling of tales for as long as a man would talk. They bribed him with drinks, hung onto his every word, and didn't seem to mind if the story changed a little with each retelling. So it was with the Grahams. However, he told the story the same each time, always leaving out his relationship with John Denton.

Just when he felt their curiosity had been satiated, old Jed arrived, clumping into the house, his toothless grin spreading wide his black whiskers. He pounded Hastings on the back and shook his arm, until Hastings thought it would fall off, and then he had to retell his story once more for Jed.

Because of the reunion, supper came late and night had settled over the land long before they finished their meal. Laurie busied herself with the dishes while the three men retired to the library.

"I'd like to offer you some brandy, but my stock is completely nonexistant at present. I do have some very good sour mash bourbon though. How about it?"

"Sour mash suits me fine," Jed said. "That there brandywine was al'ays a might too fancy fer me."

The Colonel splashed a generous portion of the dark amber fluid into each of three glasses and passed them around. Hastings took a small sip and screwed-up his face. Whiskey wasn't one of his favorite drinks and least of all bourbon, but he'd drink it to be sociable.

Choice cigars were offered, and they all lit up. Puffing on rich tobacco, they sat staring at the leaping fire in the old stone fire place and busying themselves with idle chatter. All three had something on their minds, but none would venture to be the first to raise their thoughts for a discussion. It was as if they were waiting for something specific to happen before anyone launched into what each wanted to discuss.

Presently, Laurie, finished with the dishes, joined them. She stood just inside the door, her fists planted on ample hips, arms akimbo. Her father was so relaxed, she thought, sitting back in a large highbacked chair, contentedly puffing on a fat, black cigar. Old Jed was having trouble; first, he couldn't keep the cigar lit. Then, after it was burning well, he had a problem holding it in his toothless mouth. Finally, he held it in place with a gnarled, wrinkled hand while he drew the rich, blue smoke into his lungs. She could see that Bret was uneasy. He sat on the edge of a chair, glancing from one to the other, offering a word only now and then. She felt her heartbeat quicken and a warm longing envelop her as she watched him. Should she join them? She glanced toward a chair near Bret. She stepped forward, a lump forming in her throat. She stopped. She sensed their mood. Her presence at this moment would be an intrusion on their masculine privacy. They would say nothing, but she knew.

"Well, gentlemen," she said, a bit of sarcasm in her voice, "if you don't mind, I think I will retire. I've had a trying day and I'm out of sorts," she lied.

They turned, as if surprised at finding her there in the doorway, and offered their goodnights. She looked wistfully at Bret, unsure he would still be there come morning. Love and men had often been the subject of her fantasies, but she had never lavished her feeling on any one specific man. The pain of his leaving yesterday was still sharp in her memory and, now that he was back, she didn't want to lose him again.

Hastings sensed her uncertainty. How could he

reassure her? A growing desire to hold her close and taste once more the cool sweetness of her lips ached in him. These feelings both delighted and frightened him. Attachment to anyone after all these years of being alone couldn't be permitted. A lonely life? Yes. But it was of his own choosing, and he found himself sinking deeper and deeper into the trap that a gunman sets for himself inadvertently.

It was almost impossible to back out once a reputation had been established, and he was well-known in the saloons and back alleys. He squirmed in his chair, somewhat uneasy under her stare. Finally, he uttered in a stammering, barely audible voice, "Good night, Laurie. I'll see you in the morning."

After Laurie had departed the three men remained silent for some time just staring at the fire and puffing idly on their cigars. The Colonel cleared his throat, took a long pull on his cigar, exhaled ceilingward and said, "Bret, you didn't tell the whole story this afternoon, did you? I have a feeling that there was something you were holding back, and I feel sure you were doing it because of Laurie. Am I correct?"

Hastings nodded, not surprised at the old man's perceptive reasoning. "You're right on all counts, Colonel."

Jed asked, "Jist what air yuh aholdin' back anyways?"

Hastings hesitated. His past had always been so private, never shared with anyone. Now he felt a compelling urge to unveil it; to permit these men to see into the sorrow, the grief; to know why he had been on the vengeance trail for so long. "I don't really know how to say this except to spit right out. The man I've been lookin' for all these years is right here in town. That man and me have a score to settle. I knew him right off, but I ain't sure he'll remember me. He's aged some, but I'll never forget him, not until my score with him is evened."

"John Denton, isn't it, son?" The Colonel commented. Hastings nodded.

"Denton is a real bastard all right, capable of almost anything, but I didn't know your pasts were connected. I always thought Denton was back East before he came out here, in New York or some such place. You, Bret, don't strike me as the kind to settle in a big city for a long spell. Just how did it happen that you two managed to get together?"

The Colonel was digging for facts. Was he neutral? His point blank question had stopped Hastings. He had never told anyone about that day. No one here but he and Denton could possibly know about it, and Denton had most likely forgotten the episode. Expressions of curiosity etched their bearded faces. Should he tell them? Yes, he decided, it might be good to tell it to these two.

"Well...," he started, then stopped, searching for words. "It happened a long time ago, before Denton went to New York or wherever. It was during the War Between the States, the same year as Sherman's march through Georgia. Our place wasn't on Sherman's path, so we didn't feel the brunt of his march, but for all the good it did us we might just as well have been. August was hot that year. Hotter than hell! Old Mose, our one remaining slave, and me were out in the field picking cotton." As the details of the past came flooding back, he felt a sensation of being gradually transported back through time and space to that fateful day. It was 1863, and he was a boy of twelve again. He could almost feel the hot oppressive heat weighing down upon him, his sore fingers burning as he clutched at the cotton bolls and stuffed them into the long canvas sack slung over his back.

His clothes were soaked with perspiration, and every muscle ached, but he wouldn't quit. Times were hard, food was scarce and supplies could only be bought at exorbitant prices from the daring seamen who risked the

Yankee blockade to bring goods to the Confederates, making themselves wealthy in the process. His mother was depending on him, and this crop of cotton was all they had to see them through the coming winter.

As they worked, he saw a column of mounted soldiers riding slowly along the tree-lined drive toward the veranda of the Hastings' plantation house. He stood straight and rubbed a slippery forearm across his forehead in an attempt to remove the stinging sweat from his eyes and clear his vision. Then he shaded his eyes with a reddened hand for a better look. Seeing soldiers here abouts wasn't unusual. They came often seeking hand-outs or foraging as they marched. Only these soldiers were different from the usual—these mounted troopers wore blue instead of the familiar gray!

"Yankees!" Hastings shouted as he dropped the sack strap from his shoulder and ran wildly toward the house. His father, a major in the Confederate Army, had charged him with the task of protecting the plantation and his mother. The task had been assigned lightly to dispel the boy's sadness at seeing his father go, by making him feel he had an adult responsibility. However, he had accepted the task in good faith, and now the Yankee soldiers were a threat, and he intended to carry out his presumed responsibility. Not considering that he was a mere boy against a troop of soldiers, he darted through rows of cotton toward the house.

By the time he reached the edge of the expansive lawn, the soldiers had relaxed. They were lying, sitting, napping, playing cards, or otherwise taking advantage of the leisure time afforded them by their stop. Bret positioned himself behind a large magnolia tree where he could assess the situation without being seen. A man with sergeant chevrons on his tunic was sitting on the steps of the veranda, periodically expelling a stream of dark-brown tobacco juice into the dust of the walk. He was the dirtiest man he had ever seen. His tunic bore the stains of numerous sloppy meals with many layers of foul-looking tobacco now encrusted with age. His shaggy beard was caked with a mixture of tobacco juice and dust which had hardened over a period of time, making his whiskers into strings of stiff wires. A greased-stained hat sat squarely on his head, and dusty, scuffed boots with a little toe protruding through worn leather encased his feet. This was the man he would have to deal with. Bret approached him cautiously.

The Sergeant looked up. "Wal, now, youngster, where ya come from?"

Bret didn't answer, he only glanced up at the front door of the mansion.

The Sergeant followed his gaze. "Now, young feller, ye ain't agoin' in thar. The Cap'n he's got business and he don't want ta be disturbed."

Young Bret made a sudden dash for the steps, only to have his ankle clamped tightly between the Sergeant's legs and twisted painfully back until he was flipped over and landed solidly on his backside in the dust. He fought his tears, but a couple managed to run over and splash down on his already wet shirtfront. He got painfully to his feet and looked daggers of anguish and frustration at the Sergeant who was shaking with mirth at his plight.

The Sergeant, sitting sideways on the steps with his back to Bret's left, continued to laugh. Meanwhile, Bret feinted with a step to the left, the Sergeant turned to catch him, but Bret scampered past him on the other side. The speedy boy was across the porch and through the front door before the Sergeant could even gain his feet. Too late to curtail Bret's entrance into the house, the Sergeant offered pursuit, uttering a stream of curses as he lumbered after the boy.

Inside, Bret hesitated momentarily. Should he just run up the steps to his mother's room? Decision made, he dashed up the stairs just as another soldier with lieutenant's epaulets on his shoulders came from somewhere in the back of the house. As Bret vanished up the stairs, he yelled, "Hey, kid, you can't go up there!" and joined the chase, leaving the Sergeant standing just inside the door with a look of profound amusement on his dirty, bearded face.

At the top of the stairs, Bret paused once more to survey his pursuants, then determined, he made his move. He grabbed the knob of his mother's bedroom door, threw it open, and charged in, intent on defending his mother.

She saw him and reached frantically for the sheet to cover herself. At that instant the Lietenant stepped through the doorway, clasped him in a smothering bear hug, and commenced to pull him out of the room, mumbling apologies to his irate superior.

The man on the bed turned a boiled-lobster red, leaped off the bed in one lithe movement, and started for young Bret. Suddenly, he stopped. The red turned slowly to a suffused pink. He was aware that he was naked and his composure slowly returned. He said quite calmly, "Wait."

Bret's mother lay on the bed, her face buried in a pillow, sobbing uncontrollably.

The man began to dress, doing so very slowly and very methodically.

"Bring the boy in, Mr. Blanton, and close the door, please," he said gently.

His dressing finished, he glanced in the mirror, turning from side to side to make sure his appearance suited his fancy. He picked up a brush from the vanity and ran it through his hair. At last, apparently satisfied with his appearance, he turned his attention to the boy and the

62

flustered lieutenant. The latter was quivering with fear. The fear young Bret sensed went far beyond the domination of normal military discipline.

The Captain addressed the Lieutenant, "Mr. Blanton, tie the boy in that chair." He pointed at an ornately-carved arm chair.

The lieutenant was quick to obey, his face livid with shame. He produced a long-bladed knife from his boot and cut long strips of fabric from the heavy drapes which enshrouded the windows. Pushing the boy roughly into the chair, he knotted the cloth firmly about the boy's hands and legs, securing him painfully beyond escape. Bret immediately tried his bonds, straining with all the might of his angered strength. It was useless, he found; his arms and legs were quite immobile.

"You are a might curious, young man. Didn't anyone teach you to knock on a closed door before entering?" As he lectured the Captain stood rigidly at attention except for his hands which were clasped tightly behind him.

"Is your curiosity satisfied, young man? Your mother is indeed a lovely woman. You are a very lucky boy to have her for a mother."

Bret was astounded. The man spoke as if nothing had happened, like he was an old friend of the family and had just dropped by to pass the time of day. The man no longer seemed to be aware of the woman on the bed—of her sobbing, deep-wracking sobs—nor did he seem to be aware that Bret was tied tightly in a chair, struggling with all his youthful strength to escape.

The Captain strolled casually over to the large window and glanced out across the fields. After several minutes, he again faced young Bret. "Your intrusion has greatly complicated the situation, young man. I am not in the habit of being interrupted while I am entertaining a lady. I find it quite disturbing. You need to be punished for your

63

lack of manners. Your mother too. She needs to be chastised for not teaching you better. Let me see, what would be a fitting punishment for the deed? Ah, I have it. Mr. Blanton."

Was it possible that the man believed that he and his mother were at fault and had set up the whole episode merely to harass him? Bret couldn't believe what he was seeing and even less of what he was hearing.

"Yes, sir!" The Lieutenant snapped a salute.

"Tell Sergeant Blackburn to have the men line up at the door. To right the travesty this woman and her son have perpetrated, she will bestow her favors on each and every man in my command. And this boy, who is so curious about what goes on behind closed doors, will sit in that chair and watch the whole proceedings. Then he may be a bit more polite in the future and respect the privacy of others." The Captain buckled on his scabbard. "And Lieutenant..."

"Yes, sir."

"When all have finished here, remove these two and burn this place to the ground! People just insist on learning the hard way," he added, seemingly speaking to himself.

At this, Mrs. Hastings reared up from the bed, clutching the sheet over her breasts. "But—but, you gave your word," she sobbed.

The Captain turned and glared.

"My God!" Jed exclaimed.

Hastings was brought suddenly back to the present by Jed's loud retort. He looked from one shocked expression to the other. They would, no doubt, have questions for him, and he didn't feel like talking about it anymore. His emotions had been rubbed with salt and the rawness was more than he could stand. He needed sleep. Yet he

64

couldn't just up and leave them sitting here. The room was completely silent. The awesome shame associated with his revelations appeared to have stricken them dumb.

After an eternity of time, Jed said, "I knowed Denton was a no account, but it's hard tuh believe that even he could go that fer."

The Colonel was more reserved. The story wasn't finished, and he was determined to hear the end. "What happened then?" he asked.

What happened then, indeed! Hastings shuddered at the remembrance still so brilliant in his mind. By closing his eyes he could clearly see the soldiers trooping into the room one at a time. Most of them declined to go through with it, but there were a few—a very few—who relished the opportunity. The worst of the lot was the filthy sergeant. Since the sergeant outranked the others, except for Lieutenant Blanton—who would have no part of it—he was first. He came shuffling into the room, his cheek puffed out with a huge cud of tobacco. He looked at Bret, grinned evilly, and climbed onto the bed. Moments later he rolled off onto his feet. Buttoning his pants, he approached the boy, glared for a moment, then spat a stream of foul liquid into Bret's face. Laughing raucously, he turned and stomped out of the room.

Bret retched, struggled furiously until he was exhausted, but it was no use, there was nothing he could do.

They came one by one. His presence made some of them feel uncomfortable, but it didn't stop them from spending their few alloted minutes with the woman on the bed. Somehow, she had ceased to be his mother and had become only a naked harlot in his mind. It was the only way he could endure the pain and helpless frustration of their brutal use of her body. Fortunately, somewhere along the way she had passed out from pain or shame or both.

Even now he could feel the hurt and frustration of being so helpless. His eyes teared as he turned and shrugged his shoulders. "They went through with it. Made me watch it all, then they burned the place. We moved into the slave quarters, and three days later my mother died. We found her body in a cool, little wooded area down by the spring, where she and I often went to pick wild flowers. I'm sure she took her own life because of her shame. That's partly my fault, I reckon. She tried to explain; to tell me what she had done was to save our home. It seems she had struck a bargain with Denton—her body for the house. I just couldn't believe she could do that—betray my father that way—it wasn't like her at all. But then, the place was all they had, and she loved it dearly. Yet, I can't forgive her for what she did with Denton. That was bad enough, but what John Denton did to her—I think you see why I've got to kill the sadistic bastard!"

With that he left the two old men sitting beside the fire and went to the room he had occupied before. He pressed his unpleasant memories back and let himself relax. Fatigue tore at his strained muscles, and the pleasant peace of sleep was slow in overtaking him that night.

6

The meager shade on the rambling porch provided little relief from the burning sun. At mid-afternoon the sun-baked earth released shimmering heat waves, rapidly warming the air above it, and no breeze stirred.

Hastings, Jed, Laurie and the Colonel sought comfort from the scorching heat on the shaded porch. On a small knoll a hundred hards beyond the rickety, picket fence, which enclosed the Graham's land holdings, a small rabbit scurried nervously back and forth. A broad-winged hawk glided lazily in great sweeping circles, closely watching the small confused creature below. Otherwise nothing moved in the vast oven of air.

Several days had passed since Hastings' abortive attempt to provoke Denton into coming after him. Nothing had been said about his failure to bring Margaret back as a hostage to the ranch as planned. Of course, Jed was the only one who had known the details of the plan. Hastings had not bothered to elaborate on what had ensued during his recent meeting with Margaret and Hardian, and had spent the last few days in a depressed mood, mulling over the various courses of action he felt were still open to him. He had not been able to make Margaret a pawn in his little game with Denton. His attitude was changing, and desire for revenge was slowly being replaced by apathy. His confrontation with John Denton no longer carried its all important significance, and he had found feelings he didn't know existed.

The only noises to disrupt the silence were the creaking of the Colonel's old weather-worn rocker, the click of Laurie's knitting needles, and the incessant sucking sounds Jed made as he smoked his old cob pipe.

After a time, Jed spoke. "You've been mopin' around fer days, boy. Somethin's eatin' at yuh. What can we do tuh help? We're yer friends, boy. Yuh need help, jist holler an we'll come arunnin'."

Friends. He liked the feeling—one that he hadn't really experienced before. "I guess I've been a bit down in spirits, lately," he said. "I reckon I'm just waitin' for something to break. You chase something all your life and then . . . well, suddenly there's other things which I ain't never had before and they seem so much more important—"

"What to do about Denton is what has been troubling you, isn't it?" the Colonel interjected. "What you need to do is organize folks—get the town behind you and go after him. They have as much stake as you in this. More even." The Colonel's fear of Denton was as clear to Hastings as was the old man's attempt to prod him into action.

"Won't work!" Jed emphasized, tapping his pipe against the porch railing. "They're a bunch of contented cows and they ain't hankerin' tuh stir up no trouble. Denton, he's their great protector. Usin' Shane to ride herd on 'em, he's kept this here town clean of no-accounts. They know it, and even if they ain't too proud to be settin' under his thumb, they ain't agonna go lookin' fer trouble."

"Jed's right," Hastings added, "I can't ask them to help.

It's my problem and I've got to find the answer."

"You might be surprised, Jed," the Colonel said. "They are going to have to face it some day. This time of peace will not last forever. Denton has something in mind. He hasn't gone to all the trouble of raising that gang of outlaws just to keep this town free of riff-raff. Mark my word, something is going to burst one of these days and when it does, the Lord help us!" The Colonel lapsed back in his chair.

Jed stood up suddenly, gesturing with his pipe. "There's a rider acomin'!"

Hastings and the Colonel came to their feet, crowding the rail and straining their eyes against the sun-lit distance. Laurie continued to knit, oblivious to the whole situation.

The three men watched the yellow dust cloud puff slowly heavenward as it stretched out along the far summit's ridge, then swoop down the trail across the broad flat valley and inch its way up the gentle incline leading to the house. As it drew nearer the three specks on the leading edge proved to be three mounted riders at an easy lope. They approached the house at a walk. Upon reaching the picket fence, they swung down and secured their horses to unpainted pickets. Hastings stepped into the yard followed by the Colonel. Jed started to follow too, but the Colonel turned and barked in a gruff, fear-tinged voice, "Jed, take Laurie into the house." Jed started to protest but instead just shrugged his shoulders and turned to the girl.

The man in command stepped confidently through the gate. He was peculiarly dressed for this rural area. He wore a fancy, checkered, continental suit with velvet lapels. Gray spats covered his dusty, high-top shoes. A derby hat sat squarely on his head, and steel-rimmed spectacles partially masked his face. A small pistol was holstered tightly against his belt on the left side, positioned for a right hand crossdraw. All these things Hastings catalogued as he moved slowly toward the three men. He recognized the companions of the little man by their badges. They were Shane's deputies.

"I am looking for Bret Hastings." The little man spoke in a raspy voice. "Be you he, sir?" The little man was facing him. The two deputies stood behind and to the little man's right. Hastings smelled lawman on the little fellow, but he was like no lawman he had ever run across before. The gun he wore was small in size and calibre, but at this range it would kill as quickly as Hastings' big Colt.

"I'm Hastings," he replied. The calm was there and a pervading chill engulfed him. It was like it always had been when danger beckoned, and with his right hand poised, he waited.

"My name is Lorenzo French," the little man said. "I represent the Pinkerton Detective Agency and I have a warrant for your arrest, Mr. Hastings. I will have your gun, please."

Hastings was startled. The man had nerve and a great deal of audacity. Could he be serious? Hastings weighed the situation. French had not drawn his gun, but the deputies held theirs leveled—one in his direction and the other toward the Colonel. He noticed that the direct line of sight almost placed French between him and his two aides. A step closer and the deputies would not have a clear shot at him. He glanced at the Colonel. The old gentleman was fidgeting.

Hastings brought his attention back to the three interlopers. He eased his hand down to his gunbutt very, very slowly, and gingerly lifted the gun out of the holster with his fingertips. He turned the gun carefully in his hand so that he could offer it butt first. His palm rested along the cylinder, his fingers curled around the barrel with his index finger hooked lightly around the outside of the bottom of the trigger guard. As French stepped toward him to accept the proffered gun, Hastings extended his arm, letting the gun fall from his grip. The trigger guard of the falling gun dropped over the hooked index finger, and with a flick of his wrist, he held the gun in his hand fully cocked. The whole performance had taken place in the twinkling of an eye.

As Hastings performed his trick with the gun to take advantage of his position, the Colonel had reached into his inside breast pocket for a cigar. The deputies, thinking he was reaching for a gun, fired. The Colonel fell. French was now between the deputies and himself. He stepped quickly forward wrapping an arm around French and pulling the smaller man roughly against him, covering the deputies with his pistol. The deputies fired as one, hitting French in the back. Hastings returned their fire as he let French sink slowly into the dust at his feet. The deputies jerked like twin dummies at the end of a rope, twisted away toward the fence and fell heavily side by side, staining the yellow dust with their blood.

Hastings moved to the Colonel's side. The red stain had spread out over his vest, muting its gaudy colors. His glazed eyes stared unseeing. The old gentleman was dead. Hastings stepped to French's side as Jed joined him, a pained expression etched on his wrinkled old face.

"Those damn sons-of-bitches! He warn't armed. He never carried no gun, and those gun-happy bastards knowed it. They're Shane's men. I knowed the both of 'em. They'd shoot their own brother in the back fer a dollar."

French was still breathing. Each gasp was a painful effort to retain an ebbing life. Hastings held his shoulders cradled in his arms.

"Hastings," he gasped, "all went wrong. I...I

wasn't... arresting you... officially. Not a... Pinkerton man... no more... got released... over a... year... ago. Man..." His breathing faltered, then he continued, "man... name... Norwood... Texas... paid me... wanted you... d... d... dead... he..." French slumped lifeless in Hastings' arms without finishing his statement. Norwood? The name meant nothing to him. His time in Texas had not been long. Where could it have been that he crossed paths with this Norwood?

"Papa! Oh no, Papa!" It was Laurie. She came rushing and sobbing out of the house and threw herself prone across her father's lifeless form, crying hysterically, unmindful of the blood.

Hastings lifted her easily into his arms. She buried her head in the hollow of his shoulder and gave vent to her emotions. He turned toward the house with the sobbing girl bundled tightly in his arms.

"What'll we do with them?" He motioned toward the bodies with his head.

"Bury 'em I reckon. I'd just as leave let the coyotes have 'em." Jed stopped at the porch and waited while Hastings carried the weeping girl into the house.

After he had quieted Laurie, Hastings returned to the porch.

"She all right?" Jed asked, wiping a splotch of blood from the back of his hand onto his faded pants.

"I think she'll be okay. Still crying. It sure hit her hard."

They took shovels from the barn and set to work. Neither spoke. Each was lost in thoughts of his own. Hastings pondered the wherewithall of the mysterious Norwood. By the time they had finished their chore—with Hastings shouldering most of the labor while Jed stopped often to lean on his shovel and rest—the sun was a large red ball settling into the ground, painting the western sky a blood-red, edged on the underside with a deepening purple. They checked Laurie. She was sleeping fitfully.

"You'd better git," Jed said as he lit his pipe.

"Get? What the hell do you men? I can't leave now, Jed. This whole thing is my fault. If I hadn't come back here none of this would have happened. They did come here to get me. The Colonel just happened to get in the way. I should never have let him follow me off that porch."

"Look, boy, I can take care of things here. The girl's like a daughter tuh me, more'n ever now. We'll git by. Shane'll be alookin' fer them there depities of his'n when they don't show back afore long. If you're here when they come by, you'll jist make everthin' worse'n it already is. That gal's seen enough killin' and blood today for one long lifetime, and when Shane comes apokin' his nose out here, it's gonna be you or him, boy, so you git and stay got fer the time bein'!"

"Where'll I go?"

"Hell, boy, I don't know. Make yerself scarce. I'll find yuh when this has blowed over and I git that gal settled down. Now, ride out of here afore Shane gits here, and don't give me none of yer back talk."

Hastings left reluctantly. If he hadn't imposed himself on the gracious hospitality of the old man and his daughter the Colonel would be alive now. He saddled his black and rode away slowly, a heavy sense of grief weighing down upon him. He hadn't felt this bad since that night he had found his mother. His eyes filled with tears. All he had ever done was to bring grief and tragedy.

The night air was cool. A sharp wind whipped out of the northwest, bringing the first hint of approaching winter. The sky was a large blue-black dome, punctured with tiny, twinkling dots of light.

The beauty of the night was wasted on Hastings. With shoulders slumped and head bowed, his mind churned with grief, alternating with a growing flame of anger. A desire for revenge grew anew; a need to make someone pay for the Colonel's senseless death was rising within him.

Hastings found himself following the same unmarked trail he had ridden over as he had tried to leave only such a short time ago. Once again he urged his horse across the shallow stream and once again he sought refuge in that shack, this time from a storm of tragedy rather than a driving rain storm. Would it be safe for him? Would Shane look here for him? What the hell did it matter! The old mood was slowly creeping over him. Now, if Shane did come, he would fight and if he lost—well, it no longer mattered. He had rediscovered the shell that had encased him for so long. Once again the angry gunfighter was riding the vengeance trail. It was as if the brief spark of caring had never flared—had, in fact, never existed.

7

It was a pleasant day for a funeral. The heat of yesterday had been replaced by a much cooler mass of air. The sky was a limpid blue, and a brisk wind stirred the dust, occasionally twisting it upward in little whirlwinds. Grave markers, some of wood, some of stone, stood disorganized on a hillside overlooking the town, like a macabre crop springing randomly from the soil. Gathered around a freshly opened grave were a small group of dark-clad mourners.

Among the group stood Jed, spraddled-legged, sun glinting from his bald scalp. A rumpled, threadbare suit had been resurrected from somewhere. By his side stood Laurie, seemingly unaware of those around her. She was dressed in black with a floppy, broad-brimmed hat and a long, dark veil trailing over her face, hiding grief-stricken features and swollen, red-dry eyes. The parson, wind riffling his thinning hair, stood at the head of the grave, reading from the Bible. A collection of townspeople stood silently, heads bowed reverently. Among them was Margaret Denton, a tiny wisp of handkerchief pressed to the corner of her eye.

Away from the group, stationed under a spreading oak was the ever-present, brown-clad Hardian, dutifully performing his function as body guard. At the foot of the grave was Shane, a grimace of suspicion etched across his broad, dark brow.

Other than Hardian, Shane was the only one who did not bow his head as the parson read. Shane's steely eyes shifted back and forth across the heads of the mourners. He had left Jed alone until now out of respect for the dead man and the sad-eyed Laurie, but time was growing short, and he hadn't found Hastings. The preacher droned on forever. Shane's intention was to confront Jed, hopefully separating him from the girl who made him feel uneasy. He shifted his feet nervously, and a small clod of dirt slipped and fell, thudding hollowly against the top of the pinewood coffin. The parson shot him a glance of displeasure, but his voice did not falter from his graveside service. Shane bowed his head to impatiently await the end of the ceremony.

The words the parson spoke were meaningless to Laurie. They were nothing more than a steady drone like the buzzing of a bee, barely penetrating the shield she had put up to separate her from the world of reality and all its hurt. She was conscious of being among people, but the only one she recognized was Jed, and she clung to him desperately as if the hole in the ground before them might swallow her at any moment. She had retreated deep within herself, and her mind was almost blank, free of memories like a slate board, with only traces of chalkwords showing. She refused to accept the fact that her father was dead, and that these people were here to bury him. She couldn't comprehend why she was here; why the others had gathered on this wind-swept hillside, around this gaping hole in the earth. Deep down below her conscious level, the events were registering, but it would be a long while before she knew of them and longer still before she could accept them fully.

Jed was uncomfortable, unaccustomed to the fancy clothes, threadbare as they were, and to this many people and the melancholy young girl who clung to him so frightfully. He shifted restlessly. The girl was the main problem   confronting him now. She was almost like something half-dead, withdrawn as she was. His experience with women was limited, and he was at a loss as to what to do with her.

When the small clod of soil struck the coffin lid, Jed glanced at Shane and intercepted the dark man's steely gaze boring into him. Shane's presence here was for reasons other than to pay his respects to the dear departed. Shane would have to be dealt with as soon as the service was over, so he had to think of a plausible story. Yesterday, he had told Shane, when he had come looking for his deputies and had found the freshly turned graves, that Hastings had headed west. Shane had accepted that and left hurriedly, collecting a posse of sorts as he rode through town. He must have ridden all night, and his temper was growing short like a slow burning fuse.

The parson ended his meditation, and the mourners turned from the graveside and began to depart. Jed took Laurie's arm and headed for the gate of the little cemetery. At the gate Shane blocked their path.

"Bannock, I want a word with you. Send the girl on her way," he said rather pleasantly.

Jed stopped. The girl clung to his arm, unmoving.

"Can't yuh make it another time, Marshal? This here gal ain't feelin' up tuh bein' left alone jist now."

"I'm sorry about that, Bannock. Our business can't wait. Send her along," Shane said curtly, trying to ignore the girl. "You either get her to move on or she can stay and hear what we have to say. It would be better though if she would wait over there." He pointed to the spreading tree beneath which Hardian stood. "It would be cooler for her in the shade. Our business won't take long—if you are willing to cooperate."

Margaret Denton, walking behind Jed and Laurie as the procession left the cemetery, stopped when Shane confronted Jed. She could see that Jed needed help. Another glance at Hardian, then she picked up her skirts and moved ahead determinedly.

"Come, Laurie, we will walk back to town together," she said gently, taking Laurie's other arm and looking daggers at Shane. "Come, Laurie, it's all right. I think Jed and Mr. Shane have something to discuss." She tugged lightly at the girl's arm.

Laurie looked at Jed and then back at Margaret. Her eyes were glazed and bewildered. Finally, after much coaxing she released her hold on Jed and went dociley along with Margaret.

When the two women were out of hearing range, Shane said, "Bannock, you sent me off chasing the wind yesterday. You were there when it happened. Where did Hastings go? I don't want any stalling. I want to know where he is."

"As true as I can say it," Jed said, "I don't know whur he went. Anyhow he shot in self defense. Them two rannies of yer's was the ones what shot furst. They plugged the Colonel and that little dandy—shot him in the back, they did!"

"The hell you say," Shane rasped. He gripped Jed's coat front with his two hands and lifted him off the ground, shaking him savagely. "I've had enough of your tall tales, Bannock. You haven't spun a yarn with any truth in it in your life. Now, I want to know where Hastings is and I want an answer quick! Speak now or I'll beat it out of you!" He set Jed back on his heels, jarring the old man all the way up his spine.

Jed smoothed his lapels and glared at Shane. Damn, he

was in a fix. Did he have to choose between Hastings and the girl? If Shane beat him, how could he give Laurie the care she needed? Yet, could he betray Hastings? He shrugged his shoulders and said, "It's like I said afore, he rode west. Now, iffen yuh couldn't find the likes of him out thar, I ain't sure jist whur he's got tuh. Yuh figger yuh got an idee?"

Shane looked perplexed. "My guess is he went south just like the last time he left here. What do you say to that, old man?"

Shane was trying to shock him into admitting his knowledge of Hastings' whereabouts.

"Wal, now, I reckon that's as good as any which-away tuh go. Why don't yuh ride off down that away and have yerself a looksee?" He dug his hands deep into his pockets, unable to look Shane in the eye. "Course, he coulda jist took off tuh the north or east for all that matter. Which away yuh gonna look?"

Shane wrinkled his brow, puzzled. He spread his feet further apart and hooked his thumbs in his cartridge belt.

"That is what I'm asking you, old man. I'm mighty tired of playing games with you. You know where Hastings is, and you are going to tell me and be damn quick about it!"

Jed, nonplussed, shifted the cud of tobacco from one cheek to the other and said, "Wal, now, Mr. Marshal..."

Shane set him back on his feet again.

"I figger he hightailed it out south aways. More'n likely all the way tuh Texas."

"The hell you say! That came too easy. You stay put so I can find you when I come back. I'll get him, and when I do—" Shane turned on his heel and headed for his tethered horse. Before he mounted he looked back over his shoulder at Jed. Indecision marked his face. "You speaking the truth this time, Bannock?"

"So help me iffen I ain't."

79

Shane's frown told Jed he wasn't sure of this, but he vaulted into the saddle and rode hard toward town.

Jed trudged slowly along the road to town. Hell, he might jist believe me this here time, he thought. He should have told Shane to go to hell! Whup him if he thought it would do any good, but he shouldn't have taken the risk of Shane finding Hastings too quickly.

Jed reached the edge of town just in time to see Shane fording the river. A smile crossed his wrinkled old face. His ruse had worked. West he had said and then south, so, if everything went in their favor, Shane would ride east then north. Anyway, it would buy Hastings some time, but not much. Shane would find him; it was only a matter of time.

Laurie wasn't difficult to locate, or rather, Margaret wasn't difficult to find. Hardian stood, legs spread, arms folded across his chest like a cigar store indian just outside of the Bazaar of Fashion, a tiny clothing store wedged between Olmstead's Bootery and Kentucky Bill's Saloon. Jed glanced at the big man as he pushed through the door but he received no recognition in return.

Inside, among the array of women's finery, Margaret was consoling Laurie. When Jed entered, Margaret turned her attention from the girl to him. Laurie sat quietly in a wooden, straight-backed chair.

"Jed?" was all Margaret said.

"It's hokay. It'll be a time afore the lawman gets tuh Hastings, so no need to fret none. How's the gal?"

Margaret relaxed. "Where is he, Jed? I've got to see him."

"Wal, now, that there is a fine notion, Miz Denton, but jist how air yuh gonna get rid of yer shader? Shane's one thing, Hardian another."

"I'll manage, Jed. I'll get away from Hardian somehow."

"See that yuh do, gal. Shane's hot on his tail, and I

reckon he don't need Hardian abreathin' down his neck nor yer husbin neither." He hesitated. "He's at yer Pa's shack down on the river, Miz Denton."

"Thank you, Jed. I will be careful. They won't find him on my account."

Dark had settled over the land, and all was quiet at the fort. Stars twinkled but there was no moon. Margaret drew the lace shawl tightly about her shoulders, attempting to keep out the pervading chill in the air. She moved silently down the back stairs, pausing every few steps to listen for sounds which might indicate that her absence had been found out.

She had not remained long in town after learning of Bret's whereabouts. She had offered Jed help with Laurie whenever he might need it. The girl concerned her, but she seemed to be in capable hands. She had heard stories about Jed, some good and some bad, but now that she had met him, she was inclined to believe the good ones. Besides, he was Bret's friend and if Bret trusted him she would too.

She had rushed back to the ranch to prepare for her nocturnal plans. Oddly enough, Beau had said nothing to John about her helping with Laurie. For that she had breathed a prayer of thanks and decided that maybe there was some goodness hidden away in Beau's massive frame.

Outside, the cold was more penetrating, and she adjusted her shawl again as she made her way toward the palisades which formed the rear wall of the fort. A dark figure stepped from the shadows and took her arm.

"Mrs. Denton?"

She froze, fear icing her spine! Then she relaxed.

"Bobby Jessup, you gave me a fright."

"I'm sorry Mrs. Denton. I didn't mean to frighten you."

"It's all right, Bobby. Women are that way. Did you

have any trouble?"

"No, ma'am. The others are always willing to swap guard duty, especially if it's at night. They like to sleep, you know." He took her hand and guided her quietly toward the small gate in the rear wall.

"No one was suspicious were they? I mean about you asking to stand night guard duty here?" she asked.

"Oh, no ma'am, They think I'm just—a kid," he said, bowing his head. He opened the gate and they slipped through. "The horse is over here." They hurried across the hundred yards of open ground to a cluster of trees which hid a shallow, dry stream bed. The shallow stream course began here and opened into a deepening gorge which water had carved into the hillside. The small arroyo eventually opened onto the lowland below and into another, little-used trail leading toward town.

Margaret peered at Bobby through the dim light. He was standing there so uncertain of himself, holding the reins of a saddled horse. The boy couldn't be more than sixteen, she thought, but he is the only one here I can trust. It had only been a few months ago that he had joined Denton's troops. He looked like a boy playing soldier, wearing his father's uniform. The brown material sagged on his sparse frame and had a gathered look at his waist where the tightly cinched belt grasped his lean body. She was taller than he. Only a boy, yet, in many ways, a man. She bent forward slightly and kissed him on the cheek. "I'll be back before dawn," she whispered.

Still blushing he helped her into the saddle, and she was off, riding carefully down through the ravine.

Hastings was immediately awake—alert and listening. Cautiously, he groped his way in the darkness toward the door, gun in hand. Running water in the stream and mingled voices of night creatures were the only sounds.

Then, very clearly, the plodding hooves of a single horse drowned out the other noises. He moved to the window to peer out, but the darkness was complete. The horse drew nearer and stopped.

"Bret?" A soft voice called uncertainly.

He opened the door and stepped out onto the porch. The girl on the horse slid to the ground and ran toward him, but stopped just short of the porch.

"Mrs. Denton, what are you doing here?" he asked, all senses alert.

"Bret, I had to see you; to know that you are all right. I heard about the shootings. Jed said you weren't hurt, but I had to see for myself." She stood hesitantly in the yard just off the porch.

Hastings searched the darkness beyond the immediate yard. Moments passed. At last satisfied that Hardian had not followed her, he stepped into the yard and moved close to her. They stood just inches apart looking into each other's eyes. Then, suddenly, as if on signal, they merged. He held her tightly, crushed her against him and tasted her lips. At first she stood stiffly not responding, then her lips softened against his and, like a puppet with broken strings, she folded against him. An eternity later he pushed her away.

"I'm sorry, Mrs. Denton," he mumbled. "I don't know what made me do that. I shouldn't have. You're a married woman!"

She smiled at his naivete. "Not Mrs. Denton— Margaret, please," she whispered. "Hardian beat you. That was my fault. I've got to help you if I can."

"You shouldn't have come out here. What if John finds you're gone?" Hastings asked.

"He won't," she replied with confidence. "Bret, you have to leave here—now! Tonight! Shane is going to find you eventually."

83

"Don't worry about Shane. I'll take care of him when the time comes," Hastings replied nonchalantly.

"Bret, it's not just Shane." She took his hands in hers. They were cold. "I think John is beginning to suspect something about you, and if you do shoot Shane, John will kill you for sure. I know him, Bret. He's ruthless. It would be best if you would go back to wherever it is you came from before it's too late."

"Best for who?"

She didn't answer his query, only pleaded, "please, Bret, go! I can't stay here any longer. I've got to get back before it gets daylight or I will be missed for sure. So. won't you, please, listen to me?"

He ignored her plea. "I'll ride back with you."

Her further protestations fell on deaf ears, and once the black was saddled, they rode north. Margaret pouted.

At the rear entrance to the fort, after a careful investigation of the situation, he turned her over to the keeping of the young soldier who had met them at the gate. Margaret turned with a last plea and wistfully asked again, "Please, Bret?"

"I'm sorry, Margaret, I can't." Turning before she could say more, he ran to his horse and headed him down the trail through the ravine. A strong desire to look back at her came, but he forced his attention to the trail ahead.

By the time he reached the flat lands, the first gray streaks of dawn were lighting the eastern sky. There wasn't time to ride back to the shack. He'd have to find a new hiding place. Turning the horse north toward the wooded piece of land, which lay in a low area at the confluence of the main stream and a tributary, he began his ride. Once in the trees, he found a secluded place, blocked from view by dense underbrush, and picketed his horse. He rolled out his blankets in a nearby brush-choked wadi, and stretched out to sleep.

"Howdy, Bret-boy. Now, don't go and move. I don't want to shoot you, old friend." The voice had a jovial tone, but Hastings recognized the sinister undertone.

Hastings sat up and turned slowly, being careful to keep his hands in plain sight. "Tuck, it had to be you, didn't it? How'd you find me?"

Johnson laughed. "You ain't so hard to locate. Not at all like Shane lets on. After we closed up the gaming tables, I figured I'd take me a little ride. Kind of breathe in some of this night air. Now, who do you suppose I see when I get out of town aways? Yep, that elusive badman—killer, if you listen to the local gossip—ridin' along with the Captain's Lady. Now, Marshal Shane, he wants real bad to set his hands on you, Bret-boy. He set a right nice price on your head, so ole Tuck says to himself, here's a chance to collect a new stake and save ole Bret-boy from gettin' shot all at one time. Of course, they'll hang you if the town's sentiment means anything, but then, money's money, so I tagged along behind you. Sure enough, you took the Captain's Lady home, and here we are."

"Tuck, it looks as if you've got me this time."

"Sure enough, Bret-boy. You saddle that hoss, and we'll go find the Marshal. I reckon he'll be mighty proud to part with that reward money."

While Bret saddled the black, Johnson collected Hastings' pistol and rifle.

"Say, Tuck, this sure is a hell of a way to end it."

"So it is, Bret-boy, but hell Shane would have got you in time. Me, I just figured I'd beat him to you so I could collect that prize. You ain't aholdin' it against me are you, Bret-boy? Shucks, a man's gotta make a livin'. You had your chance to get out of here for good and you didn't take it!"

Riding close behind Hastings, Johnson—slumped in

the saddle with his eyes half closed—leveled Hastings' rifle loosely at his back. Thus the two rode slowly toward town; the captive looking tired and distraught; the captor appearing to be nearly asleep as his horse plodded slowly down the trail.

8

"Carlyle!" Shane yelled.

The deputy sat up, rubbing sleep-filled eyes.

"Saddle and ride out to Denton's. Tell John I've got Hastings and I'm going to hang him tomorrow."

"Now?" The deputy asked, questioning the late hour and what disturbing Denton at this time of night might bring. He eyed Hastings with contempt.

"Yes, now!" Shane growled back.

Carlyle shuffled out of the cell he'd been sleeping in.

After Carlyle left, Shane ushered Hastings into a cell. Back in his office Shane moved over to the potbellied stove and tossed three chunks of wood onto the glowing coals and almost instantly a fire was blazing warmly. Shane grumbled to himself about Denton's lack of respect as he shed his shirt and boots. He blew out the lamp, lay back on his cot, and was instantly asleep.

Shane awoke with the sun in his eyes, swung his feet to the floor, and pulled on his boots. Stretching his arms and yawning, he went about his morning ablutions of dressing and shaving. As he examined his smoothly shaven face, he made faces in the mirror, then carried the basin to the door and threw soapy water into the dusty street.

Carlyle was asleep on the bench outside. Obviously,

Denton had accepted the news without comment. Shane shrugged, smiled to himself, re-entered the office, donned his shirt, smoothed his hair into place with his hands, and left the office.

Shane walked the short distance to Dale's Cafe. Ed Dale had died several years before Shane had arrived in Northgate, but his wife, Mabel, was making a comfortable living from the cafe. She was an excellent cook, and Shane ate most of his meals there.

"Good morning, Mabel," he said to the plump woman bending over a stove in the small kitchen in the back. A wisp of gray-streaked hair hung limply over one of the woman's shoulders from the carefully created bun at the back of her head.

"Oh, good morning, Marshal. The usual?"

"Yes, I think so," Shane said. "It sure is a beautiful morning isn't it?"

"'Tis at that, Marshal. Sometimes I wish I didn't have to spend all my time here."

"Surely, you can get out once in a while. You don't have to keep this place open all the time."

"If I did that, what would the hungry ones like you do, Marshal?" She set a plate of yellow eggs, crisp bacon and browned potatoes along with a steaming cup of coffee before him.

"Hmm, that sure looks good!" He ate in silence as the woman continued her preparations for the coming day. The hanging to take place later occupied his mind. In all of the stories he had read as a boy, the villians were hung at dawn. It was a little late for that. Hastings would hang at noon—that way there would be more people in town. The more to see him hang the better—in fact, he might even pass the word, and what better way to spread the news than to tell this woman? A good many of the local citizens patronized her cafe. He dropped a gold coin on the table.

"Say, make up a plate for my prisoner, Hastings, will you? Make it a good meal. It'll be his last, because I'm going to hang him at high noon today!"

Shane carried the steaming plate of food back to Hastings, pleased with his decision and a bit anxious to put it into action. Forcing himself, he sat at his desk and busied himself with the paper work that had accumulated in the past few days.

At a few minutes before noon, Shane rose and went back to the cell block. He tied Hastings' hands securely behind him and marched the prisoner outside and down the street toward the waiting gallows. A large crowd had already gathered. Not as large as Shane had hoped for, but there were at least twenty. He scanned the group for signs of Denton, but not a brown uniform could he see. Disappointment waxed then waned as he viewed the people clustered about in groups, talking. As Shane and his prisoner approached, the people grew silent and every eye was fixed on Hastings.

Shane smiled as he pushed his way through the crowd and up the steps to the platform. Carlyle helped him place Hastings over the trap door. Then Shane fitted the hangman's noose over Hastings' head and drew it up tight, leaving the large knot resting on his shoulder. Shane glanced at the crowd. They were waiting breathlessly. Today, the people would see a real lawman in action. Today, they would know who their true leader and guardian really was. A glance down Main Street for the last time abated hopes that Denton would be riding, since there was not a man in sight beyond the fringe of this little group. As he turned to face Hastings, he smiled again.

"Any last words, Hastings?"

Hastings looked at him but said nothing.

When Hastings made no reply to his query, he turned and descended the steps of the platform. Still smiling he surveyed the crowd once more as if to say, this is he, folks, the murderer, and today I'm going to end his life. There was still no sign of Denton on the horizon. Well, must be he isn't coming. Shane decided. Well, best get on with it. He moved on toward the lever that would release the trap door, freeing Hastings' weight which, in turn, would supply the force necessary to snap his neck. Shane was within three feet of the lever when a voice from the crowd called out:

"Hold on there amight, Marshal, don't be in such an all-fired hurry to stretch that gent's neck!"

Shane paused. On the surface the tone of the words was friendly enough, but he felt, rather than heard, a certain underlying warning in the command issued from the midst of the crowd. The voice was familiar, but he couldn't place it. Several faces passed through his mind, but he couldn't associate any of them with the voice. Facing the crowd, he searched in vain for the one who had taunted him. Frustration began to show as he surveyed, one by one, each face in the crowd. Then, as if those who stood there could collectively read his mind, they parted toward either side of the gallows, revealing a tall, lanky man slouched and facing Shane. His black hat was pulled low over his forehead, masking his heavy-lidded, somnolent eyes. The man was bent forward at the waist, his left foot extended forward, his right set back.

"Johnson," Shane said disgustedly, shaking his head. "What's troubling you? You got the reward money for bringing Hastings in." Shane paused for a minute, scratching his head behind his right ear, sincerely puzzled.

"You can't be a friend of his, Johnson. After all it was you that brought him in. Surely, you can't have anything against hanging this man!" Shane jerked his thumb over his shoulder to indicate Hastings. "Don't you want to see him hang for those four killings, and God knows how many more?"

"Well, now, Marshal, maybe you got a point there, but ole Bret-boy here ain't never had a trial yet."

"Trial? You, of all people, Johnson, are calling for a trial?" Johnson wasn't exactly a law abiding citizen. A trial would be in his interest only if he were to benefit from it. His interests weren't involved here, so why was he butting in? "Hastings needs no trial. Everyone here knows he's guilty—guilty of murdering two of my deputies, Ike Henry, and old Caleb Taylor, and I believe he was also reponsible for the deaths of Lorenzo French and Tatum Graham."

A murmur rumbled through the crowd.

"That a fact? Well, now, Marshal, maybe you're right—and maybe you ain't. Don't make me no difference," Johnson said, changing his tack. "There is somethin' astickin' in my craw though, Marshal."

Shane frowned. Johnson had gained his mistrust the first time he had seen him. The man's actions couldn't be interpreted accurately. One never could be sure when Johnson was serious or when he was clowning. Most of the time Johnson seemed to be a sleepy buffoon, and it had taken Shane quite awhile to find that Johnson wasn't exactly what he appeared to be. That was because Shane had been too willing to accept the man on the surface. It had been easier to ignore him and Slater and to class them as mere agitators and no serious threat to him, the town, or John Denton. Denton apparently accepted his interpretation of the situation since he had never broached the subject to him after his initial report.

Now, Shane wasn't at all sure but that under that carefully-contrived facade there might be a very clever man—a very clever man, indeed! This realization had come slowly. It seemed as if Johnson was stalling, prolonging the time when Hastings would hang. But why? Was he merely putting on a show for these people or did he have an ulterior motive? Was there a connection between Johnson and Hastings? They had both arrived about the same time, but Johnson had captured Hastings and turned him over to the law. Was it possible that Johnson was merely taunting him or did he actually have something to fear from this long, lean 'wolf'? Only time would tell, and he might as well play out Johnson's little game and see where it went.

Johnson was as immobile as ever. The only motion he made was a gentle rocking movement achieved by rolling to and fro on the balls of his feet. If anything, the rocking motion added to his ludricrous image. The motion gave the illusion that the man might be dead drunk and fighting to stay on his feet, or that he might be cold sober and waiting for Shane to do something he could disagree with and, thus, heat up this confrontation.

"What's troubling you, Johnson?" Shane asked again, slowly losing his patience. "Are you drunk?" Although it didn't show on their faces, he was sure these people were laughing at him—he could feel it! Marshal Shane was being made fun of by a drunken buffoon, and the people waited to see what would happen while this buffoon played games with him. Couldn't they see it was all just a pose, and that Johnson could be a very dangerous man? This he wanted to shout at the group, but didn't because he knew that it would only add to the delicacy of his position. Damn Johnson anyway! His little charade was spoiling his moment of glory, and he wasn't going to stand for this nonsense much longer. Johnson had pushed him about as far as he intended to go.

"Well, now, Marshal, that reward money is givin' me a bit of a thought."

"Reward money? I paid you that money last night. You can't expect to collect twice!" Shane felt rattled. What is this oaf's motive? he asked himself.

92

"Oh, I don't aim to collect twice for fetchin' Hastings in." Johnson paused, and the rocking motion stopped. He rubbed his hand over his jaw and smiled broadly. "But if you hang Bret-boy here, how'll I be able to fetch him in again for another reward? Shucks, I figured he'd be good for at least three times."

Shane shook his head and relaxed, almost permitting himself to smile. The crisis was over. Johnson was only funning him. Once more he reached for the lever.

"Shane!" It was a loaded command and it carried the icy chill of a cold-roaring wind, sweeping down out of a snow field.

Shane stopped. The warning was explicit. He turned slowly, his hands held out away from his sides. His adversary had changed. The black hat was pushed back, revealing the gunman's narrow, determined face. Johnson was crouched in much the same position he had held before, except that now his right hand was poised above his holstered pistol, and his eyes were wide open. The icy stare from the cold, blue eyes bore into Shane like a diamond-tipped drill ripping through soft shale. The buffoon was through playing games—or so it seemed to Shane at that moment.

Shane tensed, poised himself and made ready, his eyes countering Johnson's stare. Shane knew enough about gun fighting to know that it was the eyes one watched, not the hands. The eyes telegraphed the coming action a split second before that action started. Watching the eyes could give him that fraction of a second edge which could be the difference between living and dying. If it was a fight Johnson wanted, he would give it to him. He might be from the East but he had lived with guns all of his life. All easterners weren't dudes like many of the westerners wanted to classify them. Shane had won numerous medals and trophies for his expertise with a pistol, and those awards had come to him in some of the top shooting contests in the country, against some of the best marksmen of the day. Shane was confident.

"I'm serious, Marshal. I don't aim to see Bret-boy get his neck stretched today. You're gonna let him go so we can start huntin' him again. That sure is fun ain't it, Marshal? That's to say nothin' of more reward money." The pose was back; the rigid stance had once more given way to a slouch.

Shane didn't relax and he held his ground.

"Johnson, I've had enough of this fooling around. I'll have your gun..." He extended his hand. "...And then we can stop all of this play-acting and get on to the business of hanging this killer." Determination drove him now and he was going to force Johnson to relent or to make a play.

"You want my gun, Marshal, you got to take it," Johnson said, a trace of a smile showing on his lips.

"If need be I'll do just that," Shane said firmly.

"Haa! Shane, there ain't no man big enough to take this here gun away from ole Tuck, least of all the likes of you. The only way you get this gun is when I'm a dead man. That ain't likely since I don't see no posse backing you up."

"You're only one man, Johnson. I don't need a posse to take you. And if I need to plug you to take your gun, that can be arranged. Suit yourself."

"You ain't fast enough, Marshal!" The coldness was back in his voice, but he still posed as the sleepy buffoon. "What are you waiting for, Marshal?" Johnson taunted. "It's your play, Shane."

"Damnit! Johnson, pull that gun or shut your fool mouth and get the hell away from here!" Shane spat out, his anger roaring.

"Let me tell you somethin', Shane," Johnson said

pleasantly. "You need the edge here. Why you could grap the handle of that hogleg and start pullin', and I'd drop you before you could clear the holster!"

Shane's patience ended and he dropped his hand quickly, moving with the speed of a lightning bolt. He felt the smashing impact forcing him back. An explosion roared from a distance just before a second blow crashed into his chest. A second explosion followed and the numbness changed to searing pain. He gasped for breath, trying vainly to suck life-giving air into his lungs. The blue sky above darkened and he was aware that he clutched his gun tightly in his hand, and that he was desperately trying to pull the trigger, but just couldn't find the strength. A tornado of blackness engulfed him. He was inside the darkening cloud and was being whirled around and around. The black edge of the encompassing vortex was shrinking, swallowing what was left of the blue of the sky in giant gulps. The light grew progressively dimmer and dimmer, then everything was black.

The lanky gambler stood spraddle-legged astride his adversary, a small curl of blue-gray smoke escaping from the barrel of his pistol and wafting upward. Carlyle, unnoticed, had disappeared completely during the commotion. After Johnson was sure that Shane was out of action, he turned and looked over the crowd and holstered his gun. The townspeople stood unmoving in shocked, unbelievable awe. That someone could, and would, shoot down Marshal Shane right before their very eyes was incomprehensible.

Johnson moved quickly. In two long steps he was on the platform at Hastings' side, producing a broad-bladed Bowie knife from somewhere beneath the long, swallow-tail coat. Two quick flicks of his wrist, and the severed noose lay at Hastings' feet, the cut-end still dangling from the crossbar above.

As he sliced at the ropes binding Hastings' wrists, he said in that jovial voice of his, "Howdy, Bret-boy. You weren't amight worried, were you? There wasn't any need to fret none, ole Tuck ain't going to let an old friend stretch out a rope with his neck. Now, you trot down to the marshal's office and get your gun, and I'll pick up our horses at the livery. You meet me at the ford, before these gents take it into their heads to do somethin' to me and you."

"Thanks, Tuck," Hastings said as he jumped from the platform and ran in the direction of the marshal's office. Inside, he found his gunbelt and strapped it on, quickly checking the loads. He made his way back to the ford, deciding at the last moment to cut between the buildings and avoid the people who had now gathered around the body of Shane. The shots had brought others running from the stores, saloons and other business establishments along the town's two streets. It would only be a matter of time before someone, realizing the potential glory of motivating this mob to action, would take the lead and a posse would be after them. Beyond the buildings, Johnson waited, slumped in the saddle on his white horse, holding the reins of Hastings' impatient black. Johnson seemed as unconcerned as a young lad waiting patiently for his lady love so that they might commence a leisurely Sunday ride. Hastings vaulted into the saddle, and the two rode across the river, not pushing their horses hard, but urging enough speed from them to put some decent distance between them and the town.

"Why'd you do it, Tuck?" Hastings asked as they slowed their horses and rode side by side, eastbound along the dusty trail.

Johnson looked at him from beneath the tilted hat brim and smiled. "For the money, Bret-boy. What else? I figure I can hand you over to Denton for a tidy sum."

Hastings said nothing, deeply contemplating what Johnson had said. Presently, he glanced at the gambler, pushed his hat to the back of his head, tugged at the tip of his mustache and said, "Hell, Tuck, this is ole Bret-boy you're trying to buffalo. You know better than that. Your scalp is gonna be worth more to Denton than mine is, now that you shot his hand-picked lawman. Did you think about that before you bought into this?"

Johnson shrugged. "Yep. Figured I owed you an honor. Seen my chance so I took it. We're even, old friend!"

"Shit!" Hastings spat. "You never did anything but what you gained from it. You might have felt a bit honorbound but you had more cause than an old debt to repay. Oh, hell, forget it. It's done and that's all that matters. The why of it don't count much, anyhow."

"Well, now, Bret-boy, you put it that way, I guess I owe you an explanation. I've got to admit that Slater had a price on Shane's head—a small one," he said, holding his thumb and forefinger a half-inch apart. "Most of all, though, I see you've got a notion to do Denton in for some reason. Whatever it is, it sure has got your tail up in the air and damened determined. Well, now, ole Slater, he's got a price on Denton too, but he says I've got to wait until Denton comes into town before I collect it. Denton, he don't come into town much."

Johnson paused to dig a bottle out of his saddle bags. He tilted the bottle and took a long pull, then offered it to Hastings as he wiped the back of his free hand across his mouth. Hastings declined the bottle. Johnson shrugged and took another drink.

"Slater says," Johnson continued, "that I've got to get Denton first, then Hardian and Burton or all three at one time if I want to collect the full toll. No Hardian or Burton first, says Slater, that would give ole Denton too much of a warning and lots of chance to get his army together and come ahowlin'. I ain't one to question the man with the money so I play along, after all he's payin' my expenses, and a might handsome they are. But on the other hand I'm gettin' tired of this place and I have a hankerin' to move on. So I'm lookin' for some way to hurry along collection day. Then I see you're lookin' for Denton mighty hard, so I figured I'd collect for Shane and tag along with you. That way I don't have to work so hard. You and me, we can wind it up for them three soldier boys, and I can collect that cash from Slater for their scalps. Don't make no matter who does for 'em. I figure the money's mine, and the satisfaction of seein' them dead is yours."

Hastings nodded absently. The story sounded more like the Tucker Johnson he knew.

"There's one thing that has been plaguing me, Tuck."

"What's that, Bret-boy?"

"Slater, Ike Henry and your rifle," Hastings said, looking over at Johnson in an accusatory manner as he sought a more comfortable position on the jogging animal.

Johnson took another long pull at the bottle. "That one took me a spell to find out. It was Slater himself that lifted that rifle out of my room while I was busy at the gamin' tables. He was a might miffed, I reckon, about that show you put on at his expense that day in his office, so he sets Henry on your tail with instructions to shoot you. You know ole Slater don't like your hide one little bit, Bret-boy. Well, anyway, he shouldn't have sent Henry out on a job like that one. Now for sure, he seems to have forgot about it, at least he ain't put a price on your head."

It was Hastings' turn to smile. If Slater had set a reward, Johnson would have tried to collect it. "That's another thing, Tuck, where is all this money coming from? Slater doesn't do that kind of business from that hole-in-the-wall saloon of his."

"He sure as hell don't," Johnson said, draining the bottle and flipping it into the brush at the road's edge. The sound of shattering glass echoed behind them. "I could fib some and say I don't know, but I do. It took me a time to dig up that information but I got it! Slater's got plenty of money. That saloon is just a front." Johnson slumped in the saddle. "He's got another reason for bein' here. He's workin' on a big deal of some kind, but I ain't found out what it is yet. Denton, he's keeping Slater from goin' on with whatever it is he wants to do. I don't know how long Slater'll wait. He's got enough money to bring in more guns, but I don't think he wants to have a big blowout with Denton just now. I reckon he'll use that as a last resort if need be. I reckon he thinks if left alone, Denton'll run his course."

The thudding of horses' hooves were heard. Johnson and Hastings reined up just as the stage from Kansas City topped the hill before them and rolled past. They urged their horses off the trail and underneath a nearby tree and dismounted to give their mounts a breather.

"Say, you remember that little 'banty rooster' you shot awhile back?" Johnson asked, excited.

"French, you mean? I didn't shoot him! Shane's deputies get the honor for that."

"No matter. That's the one I mean. Feller name of Norwood down Texas way sent him after you. I had me quite a confab with that little feller, French."

"Yeah, he told me about Norwood." Hastings paused. "So you're the one that told him where to find me, huh?"

"You know him?"

"Can't say as I do," Hastings said, breaking off a blade of grass to chew.

"Well, Slater does. Him and this Norwood is what you might call partners. They're both together in this scheme I told you about. Norwood put up some of the money, and Slater is here doin' the necessary lookin' while pretendin' to only be interested in his saloon. Now, I don't know what Norwood has got against you, but if him and Slater ever get together and find out that they got a mutual dislike for you, they most likely will come lookin' for you. Now, Slater don't like you none, and Norwood must hanker to see you dead to hire that little dandy to come get you."

"That's just it, Tuck. I don't have any idea who Norwood is or why he wants me dead. In any case, with Slater and Norwood looking for me and Denton and the town looking for both of us, we are right in the middle of one hell of a spot. For that matter, things don't look too bright with just the town and Denton's army to contend with—not with only two of us, an old man and a girl."

"Hush, Bret-boy, you're makin' me a might sorry I took your head out of that noose," he said with a laugh.

Hastings' mind wandered, dwelling briefly on the problem Johnson had presented him with, then shifted to the more immediate future. Could he trust Johnson? Was he with him all the way or was he looking to take advantage of him and Jed. Jed! Could he trust Johnson enough to take him to the old man's cave? Well, trust him or not, he had to do it. And he wasn't real sure he could find the cave entrance from the directions the old man had given. The cave as Jed described it was an ideal hideout. The old man had discovered it by accident on one of his foraging trips many years ago. As near as Jed could tell the cave had been used only by an indian band several decades ago.

The stage had rolled past the two riders without anyone giving them more than cursory notice. Now, the stage pulled into town and rolled to a stop in front of the hotel, and the stage crew was informed immediately of the marshal's death.

100

Slim Hopkins, the shotgun, nudged the driver, George Busher, in the ribs with an elbow. "Say, I'll bet it was them two rannies we passed aways back." Hopkins jumped down from his perch beside Busher and opened the stage door. He assisted a demure, gray-haired old lady into the street and up onto the boardwalk. The second passenger, a tall, gangling lad much too thin for his height, descended unassisted. The lad stretched sleepily as he looked over the town with some disdain. The third passenger was short but he stepped jauntily into the street. He ain't no more'n five and a half feet tall at most, Hopkins thought.

Small in stature, but a small man—no. That was apparent not only in his build but from the way he carried himself. A little cocky, like many small men—as if the world owed him something for neglecting to give him the height that other men attained. Yet, there was something more—an aura of confidence, of power, of a complete lack of fear, as if he owned the world. His shoulders were of a breadth that gave the illusion of his being as wide as he was tall. A muscular chest tapered down to a narrow waist and lean hips. It was a muscular build that even the obviously expensive clothes he wore couldn't hide. He had a bullneck, and his head, despite the huge hat, looked much too small for the massive shoulders. From the top of his expensive felt hat down to the heels of his bench-made boots, he was all man, and he made certain that everyone around was aware of it. Hopkins watched the muscles ripple beneath the dark-blue coat as the man ascended the steps of the hotel and disappeared inside.

The stranger surveyed the hotel's interior. A wrinkled nose showed his distaste for the worn, wooden furniture, the shabby carpet, and the glossy paneling. He approached the short counter and glared menacingly at the bald-headed man behind it.

"A room," he said in his best master-to-servant voice.

"Yes, sir!" Bill Kipley snapped to attention, adjusting his steel-rimmed glasses so that he could see through them. "Let's see—second floor overlooking the street. That be all right?"

The stranger nodded as he signed the book. "What difference does it matter where the room is?" he murmured. "It will, no doubt, be just as shabby as the rest of this place. For that matter, just as undesirable as this whole town—this whole infernal part of the country.... Send a boy to find Frank Slater. Tell him I want to see him—right away! Tell him it's Brandon Norwood that wants him!"

9

Two horsemen rode the river, splashing upstream singlefile. The lead rider, astride a large black horse, intently searched the wall of rapidly-coloring foliage along the west bank, seeking a familiar landmark. The trailing rider sat lax in the saddle, chin on chest, indifferent to everything around him. Long arms dangled limply from shoulder sockets. His right forearm lay across his thigh, with limp fingers lightly gripping the reins, letting the white horse find its own way.

Hastings drew his horse up short, stopping at a point where the river began to bend westward. Turning partway around in the saddle, he rested his left hand on the horse's back.

"Well, Tuck, looks as if I missed it," he said, lifting his hand to pull at the ends of his moustache.

"Good enough, Bret-boy," Johnson replied. "If you can't find it, and you know where it's supposed to be, I reckon it's a safe enough place to hole-up in. One thing, can you find the place before that posse rides up our tail?"

"I reckon," Hastings said as he swung his horse around and started back down stream. Johnson followed closely, taking his time to complete the maneuver.

Hastings rode slowly, continuing to search the west

103

bank. Now, though, he periodically shouted Jed's name.

"Hey, Bret-boy, all that noise is sure enough going to tell that posse where we are. But maybe—just maybe—they ain't found where we back-tracked."

Hastings ignored him and kept calling. A small gnawing fear was growing. Something may have happened to Jed and Laurie, and they might not be here to meet them.

A shrill whistle rent the air!

Hastings slowed his horse, a wave of relief surging over him, and returned the whistle. A moment later an answering whistle came. Hastings spurred his horse forward, splashing water to either side. Jed was standing along the bank. Edging his horse in amongst the trees and underbrush, he followed Jed into the cave.

"What yuh doin' here?" Jed asked.

"I got sort of hung up," Hastings said, chuckling at his pun as he dismounted.

"Why'd yuh bring that there no-account gambling man with yuh fer?"

"Howdy, ole timer," Johnson said, extending his hand.

"Tuck sort of got me out of the noose. He got there before you did. Where's Laurie?"

"Damn! I plum fergot fer a minute there. She's gone!" Jed said. "Got tired awaitin', I reckon."

"Gone!" Hastings exclaimed. "Where?"

"Simmer down there, Bret-boy. Give the ole timer a chance to tell us," Johnson said, placing his hand on Hastings' shoulder.

"She was afrettin' and a fussin' 'round here all mornin'. I tried tuh settle her down some, but she wouldn't have none of it. She paced 'round here like a caged b'ar. 'Bout an hour or so ago, she sent me out tuh git some wood fer the fire. We needed wood right enough, so out I went. I jist got back and was asettin' tuh saddle muh hoss when I heared you a catawallin' like a moonstruck calf. That's it, the hull of it. She jist up an' rode out while I was out gettin' wood."

"Where could she have gone?" Hastings asked. "Surely, she wasn't figuring on finding me!" He started toward his horse, still mumbling to himself.

"Wait!" Johnson shouted as he grabbed Hastings' shoulder. "She knew you were going to be in town now, didn't she? If she went runnin' off to town, I figure she's a whole sight better off then she was here. She must have friends of some kind in that place."

Jed stepped up to face the two men. "I sure don't like tuh admit it," he said, scowling at Johnson, "but this here scarecrow is right. Dadgumit, there's Ma Dale, and that lady down at that there fancy dress shop. I cain't never recall her name nohow. Then there's Bascom. He'd take her in iffen she needed. She sure 'nough is a damn sight better off then she was here. Ain't nobody gonna pick on that there gal 'cause of us'n. She's as safe as a bird in a nest there."

"Well . . . maybe you're right at that," Hastings admitted. "Settin' in a damp cave with the likes of us wasn't any place for a gal to be. I was hopin' we could find a place for her eventually. I reckon, now, we are saved that trouble. What do we do now?"

"Damned if I know," Jed said. Johnson shook his head and sat down, leaning back against the cave wall, emitting a sigh.

Hastings said, "Food is our first concern. Soon as it gets dark, I'll ride out to the confluence and see if Bascom shows. I reckon he'll see we didn't go away with anything and bring us somethin' like you asked, Jed." Johnson had upset Jed's plan to rescue Hastings, and Hastings knew it was just as well. The old man would have been too late and it probably wouldn't have worked anyway.

Beau Hardian rode at the head of a double file of mounted men, heading into Northgate. The town was teeming with people. Farmers, ranchers, cowboys, all seemed to have met here to carry out business. It was Saturday—a day of social intercourse among friends and strangers; a day for the exchange of news and gossip. The streets were lined with wagons and carriages of all types and descriptions. Saddled horses, secured at hitching posts, champed impatiently at bits while their masters imbibed alcoholic spirits, talked, cussed, fought, gambled, or otherwise passed the time.

Into this teeming mass of chaos, Hardian brought his small detachment of soldiers. He called a halt in front of the hotel along beside the horseless stagecoach which was awaiting a fresh allotment of steeds, Hardian dismounted, letting his horse's reins trail in the dust. His troop was aligned in a row facing him.

"Prepare to dismount!" he barked. "Dis-s-s-mount!"

The troopers, in unison, swung down off their horses and stood at attention, facing their commanding officer.

"Christiansen! Flannigan!" Hardian called.

A tall, sinewy Swede, blond hair partially hidden, stepped forward along with an equally tall but stocky, red-haired Irishman.

"Corporal Flannigan, take your men and search every building thoroughly. Make sure that neither Hastings nor that gambler are in town. Start on the south side." Hardian turned to the Swede. "Corporal Christiansen, you do likewise on the north side. Work your way around until you meet Flannigan's party. Leave Slater's. I'll take care of him. Dis-s-s-missed!"

The people along the boardwalk had ceased their activities long enough to watch the small detachment of troops. They were wary of Denton's men, but felt no immediate fear for themselves. Denton had always treated them with immunity, and they trusted him implicitly.

Hardian, finished with his instructions, looked up at the vivid black lettering splashed carefully across the front of Slater's establishment. He stepped lightly up on the boardwalk. The people stepped back out of his way as he strode briskly forward, ignoring their presence around him. He pushed through the batwing doors and disappeared.

Inside the saloon, there were as many people as those that crowded the boardwalk outside. They turned almost as one from their drinking and cards to quietly survey the intruder who had invaded their midst.

Hardian surveyed the crowded room, then made his way toward Slater's office door in the rear, carefully skirting occupied tables. At the door of Slater's office, he paused. Instead of reaching for the knob, he lifted his foot and delivered a thudding kick, splintering the wood around the latch.

Slater looked up from the records before him, instantly angered. He paled noticeably as he recognized the intruder. The quill pen fell from his uncontrollably shaking hand.

"Relax, Slater," Hardian said gruffly. "Where is your bodyguard?" He looked around the room as if he expected the tall, lanky man to appear at any moment.

"Y-y-you mean you don't know?" Slater stammered. "He shot Shane, and him and Hastings ran out."

"I am aware of the killing. Where is he now?" Hardian perched himself menacingly on the corner of the desk.

"I-I don't know. He just left. That's the truth! I don't know where he went nor do I care. I'm through with him. You wouldn't expect me to retain someone in my employ after he murdered our marshal?"

"Haw!" Hardian spat, standing once more.

The door slammed open and Brandon Norwood walked in. Slater looked much relieved at the arrival of his friend.

"Who are you?" Norwood asked. The stocky little man was dressed in a pearl-gray suit, complete with matching spats. A fancy, flowery cravat was at his throat. The outfit was topped off with a bowler, jauntily tilted over one eye, the color matching the suit. He carried a black walking stick with a large silver knob which was fashioned into a head.

Hardian looked him over. Uninterested in the stranger, he turned his attention back to Slater.

"My good man, I asked a question of you and I demand an answer!" Norwood said, annoyed at the snub.

"It's really none of your concern," Hardian replied in the same casual manner. "I have business with Slater and when I'm finished I intend to leave, providing Slater can't help me."

"No doubt, it was you who smashed the door lock. You have your nerve, big man, breaking your way in here. Slater is my partner so whatever business you have with him is my affair also. Do you understand me?"

"My business is with Slater, and you are not a part of it—partner or no. If you persist, you do so at your own risk!"

"Bran," Slater said in a breaking voice. "This is Beau Hardian—you know, the one I told you about—one of Denton's men."

"Oh, yes. So you are the ruffian who is so free with his fists. I'm not afraid of you, big man!" Norwood sneered, standing on tiptoe and staring Hardian in the chin. "I may be small in size, but I warn you, where I come from, men respect my skill in hand to hand combat. Should I interpret your last statement as a threat? For if it was I will deem it an insult and thrash you properly!"

Slater cowered back against the wall. Norwood is a damn fool, he thought, to challenge Hardian.

Hardian looked at Norwood and roared with laughter.

Norwood glared, his face livid. This man dared to laugh in his face. He flipped his cane so that he held the lower end in his hand, the knobend in a menacing position. He raised it quickly and struck a mighty blow, bringing the silver knob down in a great swinging arc.

Hardian sidestepped the blow, but not quickly enough. The knob crashed into his shoulder just above his collar bone, numbing his arm and filling the skin with pinpricks of pain.

With no change of expression, Hardian stepped forward and grasped Norwood's cane, his left arm hanging limply at his side. Gripping the cane firmly, he extended his thumb out parallel along the shiny black surface and broke the walking stick as if it had been a tiny, brittle twig.

Norwood, astounded, was temporarily unable to move. An expert with the cane, he had beaten men as big as Hardian into submission countless times without any extra effort. The first blow of his expertly wielded cane wall all it took. There was no fight left, and they were at his mercy, but not this time. The big man had not even flinched, yet his arm was paralyzed—that much was evident.

Hardian's large hand gathered Norwood's coat lapels in a crushing grip, and lifted him off his feet. The arm may have been numbed, but he had some use of it. His open palm cracked against Norwood's head, snapping it sideways, pausing long enough for Norwood to right his head before he backhanded the other cheek. He kept up this slow, humiliating punishment until Norwood's face glowed an angry red, and tears spilled from his eyes. Then Hardian released him.

Norwood stood dazed for a moment, his ears ringing.

"Hardian, the next time you come to town, you had better be wearing a gun for I am sure as hell going to kill you for this! No man humiliates Brandon Norwood and lives!" he screamed as he swung around and marched out of Slater's.

"You'd better tell your feisty little friend to keep to himself," Hardian said. "The next time he taunts me, I'll use my fists. Now, if you hear from that gambler, you let me know—quick!"

"Yes," Slater said, subdued.

Hardian returned to the street. Down the middle of the rutted road came Flannigan and another soldier, each clasping an arm of a young girl who walked between them. Hardian recognized her as the Graham girl, and smiled. Flannigan, the girl, and the soldier came to a stop before Hardian.

"Release the girl," Hardian commanded.

"Yes, sir," Flannigan said, letting go of the girl's arm. "I was thinking you might want to talk with her, seeing as how she was with them two rannies you was looking for."

"That's correct, Flannigan. I do wish to speak with her. I just don't want to see her treated roughly."

"But we nev—"

"Dismissed, Flannigan!"

Hardian looked at the girl. A large, warm smile spread across his face. His heart fluttered as he took her tiny hand in his and bent, pressing his lips against the back of it.

Laurie did not move. Her face wrinkled in revulsion at first. Then as the big man's lips touched her hand, she felt a tiny, tickling sensation like a small flickering of an electric shock running along her arm. A pleasant congested feeling spread out through her breast. The grim expression on her face warmed and melted into a smile of pleasure. She gazed up into his twinkling blue eyes when

110

he was once more erect. A handsome man, she thought, and so very gentle—not at all rough and uncouth as everyone had said.

Hardian took her arm gently and escorted her down the street past the staring eyes of onlookers. She found herself following his subtle guidance, the sensation of warm pleasure mounting as they walked.

"I'm sorry, Miss Graham, for the way my men have treated you. I didn't expect you to be here, and I certainly wouldn't have you treated as you *were* treated, if I had known."

"It's all right," she said. "They didn't hurt me."

Even though his hold on her arm was tender, he held her tightly and close to his side as if he were leading her along among a band of renegade Indians and wished to shield her from any harm. They walked in the rutted street, avoiding the crowded boardwalk. Now and then a wagon or carriage rumbled by. The people along the boardwalk either ignored them or watched silently as they passed.

Laurie sensed the multiple eyes upon them, squared her shoulders a little, lifted her head, and walked proudly beside the big man. She felt like a queen passing in review before her subjects.

At the intersection they turned north along River Street and made their way to Dale's Cafe. It was early for supper, and only a few people sat at tables bedecked with checkered table cloths.

Hardian seated her at a table near the rear and he took a chair directly across from her. Reaching out he took one of her dainty hands, sandwiching them between his big rough ones. His touch was a soft, delicate caress.

"Would you like something to eat, Miss Graham? Ma Dale makes a very good apple pie."

"Yes, that would be nice." She gazed into the depths of

his blue eyes. A stray lock of his ebony-black hair curled over his forehead in a small semicircle. She couldn't explain the feelings she was experiencing. She only knew that she wanted them to go on forever.

"Mrs. Dale," Hardian called softly. All signs of his usual quiet brusqueness were missing. Mrs. Dale shuffled over to their table. A broad smile curved across her chubby face. Her cheeks were rosy from working over the fire. She was a plump and jovial woman.

"We'd like two slices of apple pie and two cups of coffee, please." He was obviously happy, and today everyone was his friend, and he wanted them to know it.

"Coming right up," she said as she shuffled off to her small kitchen.

"Mr. Hardian," Laurie said hesitantly.

"Please call me Beau," he said.

"All right. I'll call you Beau if you will call me Laurie. I hate Miss Graham—it sounds so formal. I guess I'm not use to formality."

"Laurie, you're so cute," Hardian laughed. "A moment ago you were a frightened but antagonistic little girl, and now you are a princess, quite at ease and having fun."

"Oh, yes, Beau, I'm having a grand time. You know you're not at all like everyone says you are."

"I'm glad you think so, Laurie."

She continued to study his handsome face. At this moment it was difficult for her to believe that this man could beat the life out of another with these same hands which held hers so gently. Yet, she had seen the results of those beatings. Bret Hasting's condition was so pathetic that day when Jed had brought his broken form out to their farm. He only used his hands, though—he never carried a gun. Wasn't that an indication that he was less sadistic than those who settled their differences with guns? His eyes twinkled merrily in the fading afternoon light. Those others—they had never taken the time to really get to know him the way she had. He was a wonderful man, a kind man, and if his strength was unmatched by anyone, and he won his fights with little effort, should he be blamed for what happened to those who goaded him into a fight? She was convinced that it was never Beau who initiated the fights, and that he entered into battle only after he saw good reason to do so.

Mrs. Dale brought the pie and coffee and placed them on the table. Beau had been right; the pie was delicious.

"What will you do now, Laurie?" he asked, forking a large portion of pie into his mouth and washing it down with a gulp of hot coffee.

"What do you mean, Beau?"

"Well, you can't go back to Hastings and Bannock. I mean you won't go back to them will you? They are hunted men, Laurie, and I am afraid you wouldn't be safe with them. I know you think of them as friends, so I will not ask you to tell me their whereabouts. I work for John Denton as you well know. I have a job to do, and to me, what I'm doing is the correct thing. I won't ask you to understand." He paused and took another swallow of coffee. Laurie sipped at her coffee, then brushed his hand in a quick caress.

"What I mean, Laurie, is that I would like to see more of you, and I don't want those you call friends to stand between us. Can you accept me on that basis, Laurie? Knowing what I have to do and just what that involves?"

She wanted to say yes immediately. She wanted to tell him everything; why she had come into town; about the cave and the food—but she held back. She wasn't completely sure of her true feelings for him yet.

"Must you, Beau?" She asked hopefully, knowing what his answer would be.

"Yes, Laurie, I must. My association with John

Denton is much deeper and goes further back than it may appear on the surface. I owe that man a great deal—my life in fact. Even as much as I care for you, Laurie, I can't abandon him or what he is trying to do. I believe in him, Laurie. It won't be long until he'll accomplish what he has to. Then I will no longer be obligated to him. That time is something we can look forward to, Laurie, so will you stay? Will you wait for me here so that I can see you from time to time? You might even stay with Mrs. Dale. Would that suit you? I will come into town every chance I have to see you."

He cares! she thought. The idea of spending even one more day in that cold, damp cave caused her to shudder visibly. Jed and Bret would be better off without her. She was nothing more than trouble to them. The food bothered her. She'd have to see Mr. Bascom. He'd see they got what they needed—she could count on Mr. Bascom. Besides, if she went back now she might not ever see Beau again. That decided it for her; she would do as Beau asked.

"Yes, Beau, I'll stay," she said softly.

He didn't have to say a thing. She could see clearly the rapture in his eyes.

"Mrs. Dale," Beau called.

"Yes, Mr. Hardian," she answered, folding the newspaper she had been reading and making her way to their table, ample hips brushing chair backs as she passed.

"Would it be all right if Miss Graham were to stay with you for a while? She could even help you with the cafe if you like."

"Why, certainly she can stay. I'd be happy to have her."

"Thank you, Mrs. Dale," Laurie said meekly.

Laurie walked with Beau to the door. They stepped outside onto the boardwalk. The crowd had thinned.

"Laurie, I have to go now. I'll be back as soon as I can."

"I know, Beau, please don't be long."

Her hand still nestled in his. Her face was tilted upward toward his. Would he kiss her? She closed her eyes and pursed her lips slightly. She felt him let go of her hand, and her eyes opened. He stepped back, touched his hat brim in a brief salute to her, then turned and walked hurriedly down the boardwalk. She watched him go until he had rounded the corner and disappeared from view. She opened the cafe door and tripped lightly inside, humming a nameless tune.

10

Hastings spurred his horse across the narrow expanse of water to the point which separated the two streams. A large rock, stirrup-high and nearly as wide as it was high, dominated the point. Pangs of hunger gnawed at his innards. There had been no food since morning, and it had been even longer for Jed. He tied his horse to a tree, and eased himself into a sitting position, leaning back against the rough bark of a tree trunk.

Denton would be a problem. There was no way he could possibly reach him inside the fort. Denton would have to be forced out where they could meet more on his terms. The question was how to bring him out and separate him from his army at the same time. That he was going to kill John Denton, he had no doubts. His main concern was how to draw it out—make Denton suffer the way he had suffered. The town was another matter. There was no need to get back in their good graces; just avoid them until his business with Denton was finished. Easy enough for him, and for Johnson too, but what about Jed? If Jed was to go on living here, his name, tarnished by his association with Hastings, must be cleared. This could be done after his confrontation with Denton. Each problem had to be taken in its proper order. Right now the most pressing need was food. Damnit! Where was Bascom anyway?

Hastings wasn't aware of how long he had been waiting when he heard the unmistakable splashing of a horse crossing the river from the town side. Rising silently he lifted his pistol from the holster and dropped it back.

"Bascom?" he whispered into the dark. Silence was his only answer. The rider had stopped at his utterance and was waiting motionlessly for future action. Hastings slid deeper into the gloom, palming his pistol and slowly drawing back the hammer.

"Bret . . . is that you?" a quavering voice asked from the darkness.

Hastings eased the hammer back into place, dropped the pistol into the holster, and stepped quietly out of the deeper shadows.

"Margaret," he said, coming toward her and assisting her from the saddle. "What are you doing out here at this time of night?"

"It's the only time I can get away and I've been looking for you," she said, rushing into the comforting encirclement of his arms. He held her tightly against him. The old desires rose and soon they were kissing passionately. This time there was no resistance and she returned his kiss with all of the fervor he felt. Later, they stood apart, holding hands. Neither spoke. The heat of their momentary passion had melted any resistance, and they stood and stared warmly at one another.

"Why did you come here, Margaret?" he repeated. "It's dangerous for you to leave the fort. You know what your husband is capable of if he finds you gone."

"I know, Bret, but I had to tell you this."

"Never mind. You can tell me whatever it is on the ride back to the fort. Hurry, we can't waste time."

"No, Bret! It's dangerous for you to ride so near the fort. I can make it back okay."

"Margaret, I'm not going to let you ride back alone. Besides, it's no more dangerous than this is for you, so don't argue with me. I'm takin' you back. Now, let's ride."

As they rode side by side, she reached through the darkness to clasp his hand in hers.

"They have Laurie!" she blurted out suddenly.

"Who has Laurie?"

"Norwood and that dreadful Slater!"

"Norwood? Slater? I don't understand."

"Norwood is a friend of Slater's . . . oh, let me start at the beginning. John sent out three patrols to try and find you. Burton and Hardian returned unsuccessful. Sergeant O'Brien was still out looking when they came in. John was so sure that Cornelius had found you and was having trouble making the capture, that he sent Burton and Hardian out to assist him. While they were gone, Carlyle arrived with a report. It may be coincidence but he arrived just after Burton and Hardian had been dispatched by John. Anyway, he told how Hardian's men had found Laurie at Bascom's and had taken her to Beau. Beau seemed to be quite smitten by Laurie, or so Carlyle said." Margaret smiled through the darkness. "Carlyle tagged along behind them. He told John that Hardian had arranged for Laurie to stay at Ma Dale's where he could see her from time to time. John was indifferent to the news and he dismissed it as being of no relevance to him and was about to do the same to Carlyle when the old man continued his story. He said that shortly after Hardian left, Norwood showed up and forced Laurie to go with him. Again Carlyle followed. Norwood took her down to Slater's and they never came out again. John was extremely annoyed with Carlyle, and said he didn't care about the girl one way or the other. Then he told Carlyle to get out of his sight and not to come back until he had something worthwhile to report."

They had reached the mouth of the arroyo and started up the gentle incline of the alluvial fan protruding from the gully's mouth.

"Why would he hold Laurie captive? Norwood I mean."

"They say it's because he is after you, and he figures if he has her as a hostage, you'll come looking for her. Bret, promise you won't. He and Slater want to kill you!"

Hastings said nothing. They rode in silence until the stream bed leveled off and they entered the clump of trees huddled along the stream bank directly behind the fort's rear gate. Near the edge of the wooded area, outlined by the gloom beyond the darkness provided by the trees, they could see the form of a man dangling from a tree limb.

Margaret responded with a quick intake of breath.

"What is it, Bret?" she asked, terrified.

"I'll see." He urged his horse forward. "You wait here."

She saw him disappear into the dark, and moments later he reappeared as the light of the gloom beyond the trees illuminated him, making him appear as a ghostly shadow, gliding through the air. She rode a little nearer. The view was better from her new position, and she could see the baggy clothes on the man. Bret drew a knife from his belt and cut the rope. She urged her horse forward and Hastings met her halfway.

"Don't go any farther, Margaret," he cautioned. "It isn't a pretty sight. It's young Jessup. Evidently, your husband has found out about your nocturnal excursions. You can't go back in there now."

Margaret broke into a fit of crying. "It's my fault. I never should have asked him to help me. I killed him just the same as if I had put that rope around his neck." She tried to move forward. He stopped her.

"Nonsense!" he said. "You aren't anymore to blame than I am. It's just one more of his senseless killings.

Denton simply wants to warn us that trouble is coming. As far as young Jessup was concerned, he was a misfit in Denton's army. Now you ride down to the mouth of the draw, wait for me there, and I'll bury Jessup."

Margaret turned her horse eastward, still crying. The wait at the mouth of the arroyo seemed short, for soon Hastings joined her and they headed south toward town.

"Where are we going?" she asked.

"We'll have to ride past town, then ride upstream and from there back to the cave. I figure Denton knew I would come back with you, so he knows it's me you sneak out to see. I didn't see them but I feel sure that he had men waiting back there for us."

"Why didn't they shoot us or something then?"

"I don't know—unless he wants Johnson as bad or worse than he wants me. I reckon his men will follow us to find our hiding place."

"Do we dare return tonight?"

"We'll see."

The lights of town came into view. They rode past town at a good distance. The woman followed him down into a small gully where the shadows were heavier and where they couldn't be seen from the trail. Hastings sat patiently and listened. At last he said, "I reckon they ain't close on our trail. Leastways I don't see any sign of them. Most likely they'll have a good tracker on our trail come morning. Let's go."

They rode into the stream below the town, then turned and rode north, upstream to the cave.

11

Hastings awoke to an unusual noise—a noise he couldn't identify. Groping in the darkness for his pistol, his hand brushed the butt, and he gripped it tightly, hammer at full cock. Rising quietly he edged toward the long, slanted opening. The noise came again. It was different without the acoustics of the cave to magnify it. He stepped through the fissure in the rock and into muted sunlight.

Through the leaves sporting various hues of red, brown and gold, he saw the broad back of Tucker Johnson. Johnson was idly tossing pebbles into the river. The pul-l-lop of the pebbles breaking the water surface was the noise that had awakened him.

"Mornin', Tuck," Hastings said softly, careful not to startle him.

Johnson turned slowly. "Howdy, Bret-boy. Fine day ain't it? Sleep well?" His eyes had a far away look, and Hastings had an uneasy feeling that Tuck was looking right through him.

The hour was early. Even from the shaded place among the trees, the sun could be seen, still at a low angle above the horizon. Something monumental must be troubling Johnson, for he was normally not an early riser. Johnson was a night being, and he often said he really didn't get going well until after the sun went down. Johnson was a sluggish individual, moving as if in a trance during the early afternoon which undoubtedly, was morning to him. Then, as the day wore on, he slowly came alive in response to clicking poker chips, snapping cards, gurgling whiskey, and clinking glasses. One had to be a careful observer, though, for the difference between the early afternoon trance and the somnolent facade of the late hours was very slight. Perhaps trance and facade were one and the same.

To find Johnson up with the sun, wide awake with a problem troubling him, caused Hastings' suspicions to rise. He still didn't trust Johnson completely.

"What's on your mind, Tuck?" he asked, stepping up next to Johnson, and realizing for the first time that the lanky gambler was a good three inches taller than he.

Johnson tossed another pebble. "Restless, I reckon. I've been thinkin' it's high time I was getting out of this part of the country. Winter's comin' on, and I ain't hankerin' to shiver through cold weather." He flipped another pebble into the stream.

"It's more'n that—more'n the weather," Hastings said, shaking his head. "You don't get up before dark unless you got a damn good reason for it!"

"Well, now, maybe it could be a might more'n the weather. Ain't much future in my stayin' here." A broad grin crinkled his face. "Pullin' your head out of that noose has kind of cut off my finances." The grin was replaced by a look of utmost seriousness. "I can't go back to town, not with Denton looking to stretch my neck. I don't reckon Slater'll take a chance with me. Hell, if I figure right he won't know me if anybody asks." He hooked his thumbs in his belt. Hastings thought he had never seen a more dejected, pathetic figure of a man than Johnson looked now.

"Bret, did you know that Jed's horse isn't here, and Jed isn't in the cave?" a cautious voice asked from behind Hastings.

Hastings swung around. Margaret stood just outside the cave. Her dress was rumpled and her hair was a tangled mass of reddish curls made more red by the diffused light seeping between the leaves.

The realization of what she had said struck him suddenly. Last night when they came in, and he was unsaddling their horses, he had been aware of a feeling that something was amiss. In the dim candle light he had been unable to place it, but now it seemed so clear.

"He went lookin' for you last night when he thought you were gone longer than you had ought to have been," Johnson said, laying his fingertips gently on Hastings' arm. "What good would it have done if I had told you. As touchy as you are about that old man—hell, you'd have gone ridin' off to see where he went sure as anything."

"That's right, Tuck. Any trouble that old man is in is because I put him there. Why did he leave? Was he goin' to see what had happened to me? Did he want to help me? Answer me, you lanky bastard!"

"The hell with you, Hastings!" Johnson shouted in return. "You whimper around blaming yourself for every and anything that happens here." The act was gone. Johnson was dead serious. "All you want us to do is sympathize with you—tell you your self-pity ain't there. Or, maybe, you would like for us to agree with you. Would that suit you? You're so damn vain!"

He glanced at Margaret, aware of her presence for the first time. She was staring oddly at him. He blushed noticeably like a man caught with his britches down and lapsed back into his old act rather quickly. "I'm fed up with you and your damn crusade. You don't want the likes of me nor anyone else. I'm leavin'! You can go after

123

that old man if you like. I ain't stoppin' you. You damn fool! Without me you don't stand a chance against the odds you're facin'. You ain't good enough to take 'em on by yourself. The two of us, we might have done it, but you alone..." he lapsed off into silence.

Hastings stood, speechless. Johnson felt guilty about allowing the old man to ride off after him. That was what was bothering Tuck all right. But what he had said about Hastings rushing off was true, and Tuck felt strongly enough about it that he had carelessly permitted his carefully contrived character to slip. It meant little to Hastings, but he could see the gambler wasn't sure of Margaret.

"We're even, Bret-boy, for that time in Kansas City. I ain't goin' to ride with you any more. From here on out you're on your own. I hope you realize your position and get out of here before it's too late for you to save your carcass."

"Have it your way, Tuck. I'm going to look for Jed. I have an obligation to the old man and I don't need you."

"Who's agoin' tuh look fer who?" a cracked voice issued from amongst the trees.

"Jed!" Hastings cried. "You sly ole fox, I didn't hear you come up."

"Yuh weren't meant tuh. I ain't so old that I lost all of muh woodman's ways. Yuh two afightin' over somethin'?"

Johnson faced the old man. "Ain't no fight. This damn fool was all for ridin' off to look for you. He's hankerin' to get us all killed off. He ain't got the sense of a mule. I'll betcha right now he's figuring to go ridin' into town big as you please and ride out with that Graham gal in tow. He figures his hide is tough enough so he won't get shot-up none. Maybe he figures these soldier boys can't shoot

124

straight enough to hit him." Johnson paused to light a cheroot.

Hastings smiled. Johnson was coming through more clearly now, but he still had a lot to learn about his long-legged, lanky friend. Margaret stood transfixed, afraid to speak.

"Wal, he might be a damn fool right enough," Jed said. "But we gotta go git that there gal." He moved off toward the cave, leading his horse. Hastings shrugged his shoulders, took Margaret's arm and followed the old man. Johnson ambled along behind.

Jed stripped his horse and commenced to rub it down while the others stood and watched. Jed remained silent for a long while, then he said, "When yuh didn't come back last night, when I figgered yuh should of..." His horse's right rear hoof drew his attention and he stopped talking. "I figgered one of two things happened. Either Bascom didn't show or yuh got yerself in trouble again. Whichever it was, we had tuh eat sos I went tuh see Bascom and fetch us some grub."

"You're as much a damn fool as Hastings. Neither one of you has sense enough to know when he's licked," Johnson said as he leaned back against the cave wall, rolling his cigar between thumb and forefinger.

Jed scowled at him. Turning his back to the three he went on with his grooming and his story.

"I got the feed sack. By the time me'n Hank chawed the fat awhile, it was as light as the inside of a candle-lit church. Hank, he reckoned I might as well wait 'til dark." Jed extracted a bottle from his saddle bag. "Brang yuh a little somethin' fer that raw throat of yers, Slim," he said, extending the whiskey toward Johnson.

Johnson's eyes lit up. A smile crossed his eager face, and he pulled the cork out with his teeth, tilted the bottle and drank until tears welled in his eyes. Some of the whiskey dribbled over his lips, and he wiped it away with the back of his hand.

"You can't be such a bad sort after all, ole timer," Johnson said affectionately.

Bannock smiled and continued his story. "Good thing I stayed with Bascom. We played checkers some. Had a drink er two." He grinned broadly, cognizant of their growing curiosity. "Then along about mid-mornin' these four hard-cases come ridin' in, four abreast. They headed straight for Slater's place and go inside. Gunslingers, the hull lot of 'em. That's when I sent Bascom down tuh git that there bottle and a little news." Finished with the horse the old man limped over to his pallet and eased himself down, moaning with the physical pain generated by protesting, aging joints.

"Well, seems Norwood'n Slater figger Hastings, here, will come arunnin' tuh get that gal. So they is ready fer his comin'. One of the two of 'em invited that there reception committee. Hank wouldn't say much about how she was, but they got her locked up in a storage room in the back." Bannock stopped and glanced at Hastings, waiting for a reaction.

The silence roared as Hastings' mind leaped from one thought to another, seeking a way to answer Norwood's obvious challenge. They knew Bascom was his contact in town, and if Bascom knew, then Hastings also would know.

"We're goin' in tonight!" Hastings said.

"Who are the we you are talkin' about?" Johnson asked. "You go ridin' into that place knowin' what you know about their strength, and I know fer sure you're a damn fool!" He puffed on his cigar.

"I'm goin' in and get her, tonight! I don't know just

126

how right now, but I'll find a way. Are you with me, Tuck?"

"You're not serious about this are you?" Johnson asked. Then he added, "Hell, no! I ain't with you. I told you that before. There ain't any future in goin' in there. They ain't gonna hurt that gal. Ruffle a few of her feathers maybe, but they ain't gonna hurt her none. They're settin' a trap for you. Besides I can't collect a fee for killin' my boss, now, can I? Like I said before, it's high time I was ridin' on. I've been here too long as it is."

"That's right, Tuck!" Hastings spat out, his anger rising, "Run the hell out. I'll do it alone! I ain't as helpless as you make out I am. I don't need you or anybody. Now, you climb up on that white, sway-backed nag of yours and you ride the hell out of here! Go south so you can keep warm. Sell that gun to somebody that'll pay good for it! Now get before I decide to make you earn some of Slater's money!" Hastings crouched, his hand hovering over his gun.

Johnson's eyes narrowed, but he ignored Hastings' challenge. He merely straightened up and looked coldly at him. He tossed the now dead butt of his cigar away in disgust.

"You do everything the hard way," Johnson said crisply. There was no pretense now. "The odds of your living to see another sun rise are mighty small. Hell, I don't know how you managed to live this long." Johnson pushed his hat firmly down on his head, saddled his horse and left.

They could hear the splashing of his horse's hooves in the river as he rode away.

"Should you have done that, Bret?" Margaret asked. "Don't we need him?"

"Yes," Hastings said calmly, "we need him."

"Mebbe not," Jed said. "A man never knows when the likes of Tucker Johnson will turn on him. I say we're a durn sight better off without him."

"Could be," Hastings said, all anger gone. "Let's get some rest. We have a busy night ahead of us."

12

Darkness came and Hastings grew impatient to leave. No plan had been formulated. Undoubtedly, it was a trap set to snare him, and they knew he would come after the girl. Jed was anxiously saddling the horses. There was the two of them against four hired guns, not to mention Norwood and Slater. Norwood was an unknown factor. They had never met that he knew of. Slater, though, he could discount. Slater was too much a coward to mix in a fight where he would be in any kind of danger. Five then, at most, they would have to face. The time that he and Tuck had taken four in Kansas City drifted through his mind. Of course, they hadn't been professionals, but they had held drawn guns. He hadn't counted on Johnson backing out at the last minute. But he had just when Hastings thought he was beginning to understand Johnson. Tuck could have made the difference in what was to come. Well, no use fretting over what was done.

"Let's ride," Jed said leading the horses forward.

They rode slowly, following the tributary and taking the back trail into town. Stars shone brightly, but there was no moon, and the lights of town gleamed through the darkness. Hastings called a halt near a stand of trees. Only three in number, the trees looked to be growing out of a mound of rocks twenty yards from the trail.

129

"We'd best leave the horses here," Hastings whispered. They dismounted and tied their mounts loosely to the trees. Jed pulled his shotgun from its sheath along the saddle, and the two men made their way quietly along the back of the buildings, being especially careful to keep to the shadows. He sensed an unusual tenseness in Jed, an over-eagerness and a thirst for adventure, he surmised.

The two men stopped behind Slater's. The saloon had no rear door, but there was a side door not too far from the back of the building. Hastings edged along the side, keeping in the shadows and being careful not to accidently knock over any of the barrels or boxes which littered the alley. Jed, like a shadow, followed close behind. Hastings stepped up on the second and top steps and slowly inched the door open. The saloon's interior was brightly lit after the dark of the night. Business wasn't good tonight, only six men deeply engrossed in a poker game occupied a table near the front of the establishment. Three others stood along the bar on the far side of the room. Otherwise, the place was empty.

The three at the bar Hastings recognized as the gunmen hired to spring the trap on him. It certainly didn't look like a trap—but then, traps were not supposed to appear to be what they were. Maybe they were earlier than expected. Sure, he thought, the most logical time to expect them was in the early morning hours when there would be few people about. Norwood and Slater were anticipating his arrival in the wee hours of morning. Hastings smiled, pleased at his over-anxiousness which had brought him here early in the evening. He stepped down and motioned for Jed who was watching the alley entrance to come closer.

"Give me time to get in the front door, then you come in this way. We'll have 'em in a crossfire, and I reckon they won't want to argue with that scatter gun of yours."

130

Hastings sauntered nonchalantly out of the alley and along the boardwalk, no longer attempting to hide his presence. Confidence bubbled with every step. He'd catch them in their own trap. He paused at the front doors, drew his gun, cocked the hammer, and stepped into the saloon. At first no one paid him any attention, then gradually each inhabitant of the saloon became aware of him and silence reigned. The card game ceased. The men at the bar turned slowly, keeping their hands in sight. They didn't seem at all surprised at his appearance.

"You gents find some place else to play cards," he directed as Jed stepped through the side door with shotgun leveled. "I've got business with them three." He motioned toward the three at the bar. The card players rose, trying vainly to show that they were not hurried or frightened by what might ensue.

After they had gone one of the gunfighters stepped forward away from the bar and stood with legs spread, hat tilted back, hands resting on lean hips, eyes staring intently at Hastings.

"Bret Hastings! It's been quite some time hain't it?"

Recognition swept over Hastings. "Billy Bob Tuttle!"

"Let's see," Tuttle said, "the last time was that range war out in New Mexico Territory wasn't it? We was on the same side that time. Now looks like we'll be buckin' one another. Happens at times. 'Pears to me you didn't look careful afore you picked sides."

Hastings ignored Tuttle. "Drop your gunbelts," he commanded.

"It sort of looks like you got the upper hand this time. What with your gun in hand, and the old man wavin' that scatter gun. You remember, Hastings, how I was always tellin' you how good you were? I even figured you was damn near as good as Billy Bob Tuttle and I told you so. Ain't many I can say that about, and I still say you're

131

damn near as good as me. You got the guts to try and prove you might be better than me?"

Hastings was tempted. It wasn't the first time Tuttle had invited him to fight. He had done it often in New Mexico, especially when others were near enough to hear. His refusal each time had always been interpreted by Tuttle as fear of him and it would feel good now to shut that boastful mouth once and for all. However, he had disciplined himself. His feelings and his temper in particular could not overcome his good sense and get in the way of successfully stealing the girl away.

"Didn't I tell you fellers how good Hastings was?" Tuttle asked of his compatriots. "I reckon it would be a toss-up between you and him, Price. He's that good with a gun." Tuttle addressed the shortest of his two companions.

Hastings eyed Tuttle. They were about the same height, but there were several unusual things about Billy Bob Tuttle. First, his hair was as white as the snow that capped the Bitterroots. The whiteness of his hair gave him an almost reverent appearance, especially when he wasn't wearing his battered, black hat. Second, his skin was fair, giving an illusion that it was translucent. Close inspection gave one an eerie feeling of looking right through his skin into the flesh beneath. Third, and most striking, were his eyes. They were pale, light-gray, almost colorless. The gray was rimmed with a thin border of red. The eyes were piercing and unnerving. Hastings looked away.

"Let me make you a deal," Tuttle said. "You hold the high cards now. I'll draw with you fair and square. No need to worry none about the old man—he goes free."

Hastings felt for a moment that Tuttle was reading his thoughts.

"How about it, Hastings? Just you and me. I think maybe these boys don't believe me when I tell 'em you're almost as good as me. You want to make believers out of

132

'em don'cha? We're gonna get you one way or the other anyhow. This gives you a chance to die like a man. It's better than hangin' any day. What do you say? Want to give her a try?"

"Hold on a minute, Tuttle," Hastings said. "You talk too much and too long. I'll give you your chance to show your boys just how you fight and that you ain't fast enough to beat me on any day of the week, but first, you tell your boys to unbuckle and kick them gunbelts over here, then we'll go at it."

"What about the old man? Soon as I gun you, he'll let go with that scattergun. Oh no, Hastings, we have to even up things more'n that."

"You backin' down, Billy Bob?" Hastings taunted. "See fellows, he's all mouth and when it comes to fightin' he starts lookin' for a way out."

"Damn you, Hastings! I don't aim to get splattered all over the wall with a load of buckshot."

"Okay, Billy Bob, if you get real lucky and win this shoot-out, Jed goes free and clear. He don't bother you none and you leave him go. That's the way it's got to be or not at all as long as I hold this gun. Agreed?"

"Agreed," Tuttle said reluctantly.

"Hold on thar," Jed bellowed. "Yuh ain't aspeakin' fer me nohow. Iffen that there white-headed billy goat wins, I'll fill his side so full of buckshot he won't be able to stand upright with the weight of it."

Hastings laughed. "Shows how much faith my comrade has in my ability don't it, Billy Bob?"

Tuttle smiled.

Jed could see they were making fun of him, and his weather-beaten face reddened. "Well, damn yer hide, Bret Hastings! You go ahead and let this here loud-mouthed stump jumper shoot yer ears off. Iffen he don't I'll do her myself." With that he up-ended the shotgun and rested the stock on the floor.

"Drop your belts, boys," Tuttle said.

They obeyed quickly, giving the belts a shove across the floor in Hastings' direction with their feet.

Hastings holstered his gun and faced Tuttle, knowing that Billy Bob was fast. He stared intently into the red-rimmed gray eyes. The eyes were hypnotic—cold on the inside with a hot border which seemed to expand and contract with each beat of the man's heart. He glanced away for an instant trying to dispel the hypnotic effect. As he did, Tuttle made his move. Guns roared with a deafening crescendo in the confines of the saloon. Hastings felt a searing finger of flame burn along his side. Billy Bob Tuttle gasped as Hasting's bullet hit him dead center. The impact slammed him back like a sudden gust of wind whipping up a straw. Tuttle lay still except for the twitching of tensed muscles which were longer in giving up life than the man himself. Hastings could feel blood oozing from the furrow ploughed in his side and wetting his shirt. The burning sensation was gone. The wound felt numb. He brought his gun to bear on the other two gunslingers. Then it hit him . . . there were supposed to be four! Where was the fourth? He had been so anxious to free Laurie that he had overlooked the fact that only three gunmen were here.

"Drop the gun, Hastings, and turn around real slow." The voice that spoke the warning came from the door behind him.

Jed had seen Norwood come in after he had spoken. He turned the shotgun in Norwood's direction but there was no chance of hitting Norwood without hitting Hastings too. A step echoed behind him!

"Lay down the gun, ole timer, very easy. We wouldn't want it to go off accidently, would we?"

It was the fourth. Everyone was here now. The trap had been sprung, and it had worked to perfection.

13

Hastings cursed his carelessness; his desire to put an end to the continual harassment of his friends had led to his forgetting his usual caution. Now he had walked blindly into the trap, thinking only of quickly freeing Laurie. He was the damn fool Johnson had labeled him earlier in the day. Damnit! If Tuck had been here the proper caution would have been exercised, and he and Jed wouldn't be in this helpless position. But he couldn't blame Johnson. He had done the only sensible thing.

Norwood motioned Hastings over to the bar. They stood face to face, the shorter man's head barely reaching Hastings' nose level. Norwood's facial expression was a mixture of gluttony and glee, as if he had found that he had suddenly accomplished the improbable and was preparing to enjoy every second of his triumph to the utmost. Norwood shrugged his massive shoulders as if he were trying to position his coat into the proper place. Spreading his short, stubby legs, he looked menacingly up at Hastings and addressed him curtly.

"You don't know me do you? In fact, you don't even remember the incident for which I've spent a good number of years looking for you so that I could have vengeance." He shifted his position slightly waving his gun threateningly under Hastings' nose.

"No, I don't remember you or anything about you, except for French," Hastings replied, his mouth turning a little dry.

"I'll refresh your memory," Norwood said. "It was a long time ago in Fort Worth. You recollect any of it yet?"

Hastings shook his head. Fort Worth? It had certainly been a long time since he had been there. Norwood still puzzled him. Relaxing, the calm-cool pervaded him, and he looked for an opening. Norwood was the only one who held a gun. The others stood by merely taking in the interrogation. Hastings glanced sideways at Jed. The old man's eyes were flashing with anger. He was ready for action. Hastings looked back at Norwood. With Jed here he would have to be careful. If it were him alone he would make a try for Norwood's gun, use him as a shield and, hopefully, wrest the gun away from him in time to cover the others. The memory of the situation when the Colonel had died because of his attempt to thwart the intentions of Lorenzo French and the two deputies tormented his memory. Perhaps, he could get them to separate him and Jed. It was worth considering. Then there was Laurie. He had to get to her.

"You listen when I talk to you!" Norwood growled.

"What?" Hastings said, becoming aware that Norwood was still addressing him.

"When I talk to you, boy, you listen!"

"Yeh, I'm listenin', go ahead with whatever you've got to say," Hastings said.

Norwood smiled and jabbed the barrel of his pistol into Hastings' stomach. "I want you to remember that night in Fort Worth. In fact, you are going to remember it in detail before I'm through with you! You were in a cantina—a very crowded cantina. There was a soldier—a young soldier—sitting at a table with a dark-haired Mexican girl. There were those who saw you that night—saw what

136

you did. Fortunately for you I wasn't there, but friends painted a very vivid picture for me. You beginning to remember? Answer me, boy!" Norwood shouted.

Hastings was digging frantically for the images stored away somewhere within his brain—images that would bring back the date and the event that Norwood was trying so hard to prod to the surface. If, indeed, he had been the one in that cantina so many years ago as Norwood suspected, he couldn't remember.

Then, like a man suddenly turning a corner, it was there as sharp and as vivid as if it had taken place only the night before. The interior of the cantina was there in his mind's eye. The name was lost in a maze of time. He could see again the heavy layers of blue cigar smoke hanging in the air, wreathing coal-oil lanterns. The garbled sounds of many voices had been mingled together into nonsense sounds. Above the noise of voices, the clicking of castanets and the tapping of heels could be heard. A lithe, dark-haired girl was whirling about in an impromptu dance in rhythm with the castanets on the small stage at the opposite end of the room. The skirt of her red velvet dress—mid-calf in length—swirled about her, exposing her firm, brown thighs to a very attentive audience. He had had several drinks and was feeling a bit unsteady.

Pausing just inside the door, he had given full attention to the dancing girl for just a moment. Even now he could remember her loveliness in surprising detail. As her dance had ended and she had launched into another number, he had started to make his way toward the stage for a closer look at her.

It was then that he had seen the soldier. The man's back had been toward him but it was the man all right. The man who had made a shambles of his life. He had called out to the soldier, calling him every foul name he could think of, venting his smoldering anger. The soldier, startled by the sudden onslaught, accepted the challenge put to him. The soldier hadn't spoken. He didn't have to, the expression on his face had said it all. Here is another rebel troublemaker who needs to be taught a lesson. The soldier had risen and faced Hastings with ten yards separating them. Then the realization struck him. This wasn't the man he sought!

There was a very striking resemblance between the two, all right, but it wasn't the man who had paid the malicious visit to the Georgia plantation that fateful day. Hastings, realizing his mistake, had been ready to apologize but it was then too late, the soldier's gun hand was in motion. Hastings had moved quickly, and with a little luck had beaten the soldier.

The fight had been fair, but the post-war government wouldn't have seen it that way. He was a Southerner and it was a Yankee soldier he had prodded into a fight and killed.

The cantina had had a number of Southern sympathizers who still fought back at every chance, even though the war had ended nearly five years previously. The sympathizers had hustled him out of town. He had ridden on to Sante Fe. In time his reputation with a gun had blossomed, and he found it increasingly difficult to obtain "honest" work. That night in Fort Worth was a night he had made a mistake—a mistake that would cost him dearly.

Hastings looked coldly at Norwood. "I remember the night. But what does it have to do with you?"

"That soldier you so brutally murdered was my younger brother," Norwood said.

So that's it, Hastings thought. Then the interruption came—

"Reach for the ceilin', gents. Don't go and make any sudden movements. I ain't missed what I shot at for one

138

hell of a long time. You, Norwood, have one sixgun aimed square at your spine. If you and your cohorts don't drop those guns in one second, I'll be throwin' lead your way!"

Guns tumbled to the floor.

"Tuck!" Hastings exhaled with relief. "What the hell! You always show up just at the right time."

"Not now, Bret-boy, grab those guns and we'll hightail it out of this town."

Hastings moved quickly, holstered his own gun and stuffed two more into his belt. Two others he flipped in slow succession to Johnson. The lanky gambler followed Hastings' lead, catching them deftly in his free hand and pushing them into his belt. Norwood's gun went to Jed who shoved it inside the waistband of his pants as he scooped up his shotgun and went over to the storeroom door. After a succession of hardy kicks, the lock gave and Laurie was free.

"Give me and this here gal a half hour then yuh can do for these sidewinders and come along." Jed instructed.

"Right!" Johnson saluted the old man with his gun barrel in mock tribute.

The half hour passed slowly. Norwood reiterated again and again what was in store for Hastings the next time their paths crossed.

Hastings was trying to figure it out, but Johnson was saying nothing. The gambler quietly watched the four before him, ignoring the body of Billy Bob Tuttle stretched prone in a pool of dark blood not five feet from where he stood.

Time crawled by slowly. Hastings was impatient to leave, but over-anxiousness had almost ended in tragedy once tonight. The memory was still warm in his mind, and he forced himself to be patient, determined to give Jed and Laurie a sufficient lead.

It was Johnson who finally announced when it was

time to leave. They backed toward the door, cautioning Norwood and his men not to follow too quickly. Outside the sky was clear, and the streets were deserted. A rumble of commotion issued from the Bonanza Saloon down the street on the corner, highlighting the saloon as the town's center of activity for the night. Hastings led the way through the alley. The shadows were thick and he found it difficult to see. His thigh struck an object and a sharp pain flashed along his leg. He gritted his teeth to choke back a curse rising in his throat. A loud crash of falling boxes came from behind him followed by a string of profanity which was instantly accompanied by the muffled thump of a falling body.

"What is it, Tuck?" he whispered into the dark.

"I twisted my damn leg," came the reply.

Hastings' eyes were now more accustomed to the dark, and he could see the dim outline of Johnson trying vainly to struggle to his feet. Hastings moved quickly. Swinging Johnson's left arm around his own shoulders and, at the same time, gripping the lanky gambler around the waist, he pulled him slowly to his feet.

"Ouch! Damn! Ain't no use Bret-boy, I can't put my weight on it nohow. Ain't no starch left in that ankle of mine. It just wobbles all over the place. Leave me. Get away. Ain't nobody comin' down this alley—not while I got three guns they ain't. Now, get out of here!"

"Be quiet," Hastings rasped. "I ain't leavin' you behind. There's that old sod house out back aways. If we can get into that we can hold them off."

Straining and stumbling in the dark with Hastings supporting most of Johnson's weight, the two managed to make it across the fifty or so yards to the old sod house long ago abandoned.

The house was small—about ten feet long and six to seven feet wide. The edge of the flat roof was on a level with the top of his hat. The doorway was small, and the weathered old door hung useless by one rusted hinge. With a great strain exerted on his arms, he saw that he could enter the sod house, easing Johnson carefully through the entrance behind him so as not to put an undue amount of weight on the injured ankle.

The floor of the house was hard-packed earth and was recessed about a foot below ground level. Thus he found he could easily stand erect. Among the broken and rotting furniture which littered the floor, he found a rickety wooden chair which still had four legs intact. He eased it over to the doorway with his foot, and gently assisted Johnson into it.

"It'll take awhile for them to find guns and come after us. I'll have a look at that ankle now." He gingerly probed the injured leg with his finger tips. "I'll have to cut that boot off. I can't do much with it as it is and I doubt I can pull it off the way it's all swoll up."

"Ain't no use you stayin' here, Bret-boy. You need to get after that old man and those two gals. They need you a damn sight more'n I do. Ain't much you can do here except get yourself shot-up or hung."

Hastings drew a knife from his belt and carefully slit the boot leather down from the top to the harder leather of the shoe, then skinned strips of leather down Johnson's leg like peeling a banana.

"There's only four of 'em, Tuck. If they want to come after us . . . well—me'n you can take four of the best even with you sittin' in a chair." A few more deft moves with the knife and he was able to remove the ruined boot.

Johnson uttered a cry of pain as he tugged the boot from his foot, then the gambler leaned back in the chair, breathing hard. Hastings was on his feet again, staring into the black shadows at the rear of the saloon, holding a pistol in his right hand. The only window was a small

141

opening in the back of the house. It would be an easy place to defend.

"Tuck, we can defend this place against them four for as long as we need to," he said. "We'll just sit tight and wait for 'em to come."

"That's just it, Bret-boy," Tuck said. "We ain't got time atall. It ain't just them four. If it was I'd stick it out with you. I reckon we could take 'em if we had to."

"Damn right we can!" He paused. "Just what do you mean by more than four of them?"

"Do you hear that commotion up to the Bonanza as we come out of Slater's!"

"Yeh, I heard it. So what?"

"That wasn't any regular night jamboree up there. Listen, after I left you this mornin' I knew I had to come back. I reckon I never really intended to leave at all. I knew that you'd go ahead and try to get her out of there, so I figured I'd ride in just like I did. I guessed that if they got the jump on you I could walk in late and heist them a bit. After dark I hid my hoss and nosed around some. Well, ol George Busher—you know him, don't you? Drives the stage on the Kansas City run now and again. Well, ole George, he'd had a couple of belts of good liquor and he's tryin' to get the crowd riled up about you, Bret-boy. Seems he knew you was going to be comin' into town tonight. Now, it's only a matter of time until these folks get liquored up enough to think they could lick an army. Then they'll come troupin' down here and ..."

He thought about it. It was evident that not only could he and Johnson be killed but many of the people following Busher could get shot in the melee that would occur. These people had no part in this fight, and he didn't want them drawn into it if he could help it.

"Relax, Tuck. We'll work it out somehow. Where's your horse?"

Johnson described the location where he had left his horse. Hastings was relieved to learn that Johnson had hidden his horse in a thicket only a few hundred yards from the place he had left his black. He tensed and strained his eyes in the darkness. Had he detected a flicker or movement? He held his pistol ready. A shot boomed out of the night. A slug thudded harmlessly into the sod, kicking out a cloud of dust and debris.

"They heard us talkin', Bret-boy. They can't see us and that's for sure. I got an idea. You rustle around some—draw their fire, and I'll pinpoint the flashes and shoot at them. What do you say?"

Hastings moved around the edge of the door. Nothing but shadows of varying shades of dark gray were evident. He faked a sneeze and ducked back inside quickly. An undetermined number of shots split the night air. One struck the rotting door jamb and ricocheted into the house. Then Johnson's gun exploded. The sound was magnified greatly by the close confines of the sod hut, making his ears ring. Through the ringing he could hear an agonized cry of human pain.

"I got one!" Johnson cried elated. "It may not be as easy next time, Bret-boy. They may know what we're up to." Johnson jacked three spent shells out of his gun and replaced them with fresh ones.

A fusillade of shots illuminated the night. One bullet whined dangerously close passed Bret's ear; then there was silence. Johnson took careful aim and fired in the direction of one group of flashes. The loud smack of lead on wood was all that they heard.

"They're playin' it smart," Johnson said.

Another fusillade of firing crashed into the sod house. Johnson moved in his chair, cursing in the dark, and snapped off shot after shot, alternating first to one side then to the other side of the positions where the firing had come from. This time he was rewarded with a grunt of pain, followed by some garbled cursing that ended in a gasp.

"Number two," Tuck said.

Through the silence they could hear the roaring crescendo of a marching mob. It was still relatively low but growing louder. Busher's mob from the Bonanza was on its way.

"That'll be Busher," Johnson whispered. "You better get while you still can. Give me those extra guns and I'll hold them at bay for as long as I can."

"Sit tight, Tuck. I got an idea. Cover me, I'm gonna make a run for it." He dropped one of his two extra guns in Johnson's lap.

Johnson opened fire, slowly snapping his shots in a carefully positioned pattern. Hastings ducked through the door and dashed, bent at the waist, for about ten yards, then he dived into the dirt, rolling over and over. Shots speared out of the dark, and slugs kicked up dirt all around him. Johnson answered with twelve quick shots. Under Johnson's protective fire, he managed to make it to a wagon parked behind the building next to Slater's.

Quiet reigned except for the noise of the approaching mob. Hastings rested, drawing in great lungsful of air. When he felt the time was right, he made a quick dash for the security of the back of the buildings lining Main Street. Once behind them he ran parallel to Main Street along the rear of the buildings to an alley leading out to River Street.

He took a position in the center of the intersection of the two streets with the river at his back. The mob was moving away from him, approaching Slater's. They were shouting in drunken exuberance. Some were waving bottles aloft, others carried rifles. One man proudly carried a flag of sorts. It appeared to be a portion of red velvet curtain torn from the Bonanza's wall and held aloft on a billiard cue. Several others carried torches.

Hastings shouted. It was useless. They couldn't hear him for the noise they were making. He drew his pistol and fired into the air. No response came from the surging mob. He fired again. The mass of men slowly quieted and turned around to see who was doing the shooting behind them.

"It's me, Hastings," he shouted. "You want me? Come and get me! I'm through with Slater." He waited only long enough to make sure they were coming, then he broke into a run, going south along River Street. Cutting quickly in between the livery stable and the small tobacco shop, he ran along the backs of the buildings on the opposite side of Main Street from the ones he had paralleled as he had come up the other side.

Beyond the town, to the west, he found Johnson's white horse just where Tuck said it would be. He swung into the saddle and rode hard to the spot where he had left his black. Leading the black, he spurred the white horse back toward the sod house. In front of the doorway of the house, he sprang from the saddle, snapping off a barrage of shots at several places where he thought one of the gunmen might be hiding. Another cry of agony rang through the night as he ducked beneath the belly of the white horse, and came out on the other side, facing Johnson who had managed to pull himself to his feet. Hastings moved quickly, assisting the injured Johnson into the saddle, before slapping the flank of the white horse to send it galloping off toward the north. He swung around just as quickly, leaping astride his black, spurring it into a full gallop to follow Johnson's lead.

A rifle shot cracked behind him, and the smashing impact of a bullet slammed into his left shoulder, throwing him forward along the horse's neck. He uttered an involuntary cry of pain. The hurt was excruciating and was centered just to the left of his spine with sharp darts of pain down the length of his left arm. It was a deep bone ache completely obliterating the sting of his earlier wound. He fought to stay in the saddle as he swayed back and forth. The night was suddenly hot and he was sweating. Nausea crept upward and the world blurred before him. Desperately he tried to call for help but no sound came. A red haze covered his eyes, muting the world into a filmy, crimson sea. He leaned forward grasping frantically for the horse's mane. The pain of bringing his left arm up to grab the mane caused him to fade from consciousness for an instant. Once more awake, he locked his fingers tightly in the long, coarse hair, but he could no longer feel the bobbing motion of the horse under him as it raced swiftly over the ground. The landscape and the stars above were swimming around him, and he knew he was reeling in the saddle. He tried to right himself atop the speeding horse, but his muscles no longer followed his will. He couldn't move, and panic overtook him. The world slipped away faster and faster—then it was gone.

14

Johnson leaned low over the horse's neck enabling him and the horse to pass through the narrow fissure into the cave. Hastings' limp body was draped over the saddle of the black. His wrists and ankles were tied with a rope running beneath the horse's belly.

Margaret stepped forth cautiously. She gasped when she saw the lifeless form. "Oh, my God! Is he?... is he?..."

"He's not dead, ma'am," Johnson said as he slipped from the saddle, using it and the horse as a support. Leaning on Hastings' horse in a similar manner, he managed to work his way around to Hastings' head. Going down on his knees, he slipped Bret's knife from its sheath and deftly cut the rope that bound him. With great effort he managed to pull the limp form from the horse and over his shoulder. Then walking on his knees, dragging the injured ankle behind him, he moved Hastings over to one of the straw pallets.

Margaret watched with panic threatening to destroy her composure. Confused as to what she should do, she did nothing but wring her hands helplessly.

Dark blood had crusted over the back of his shirt and some of it had trickled down his arm, and still more had run down over the back of his head and had caked into a dark-red mat in his hair like thick molasses.

Margaret passed through a moment of hysteria and then calmly knelt beside Hastings. With the knife Johnson had used to sever the rope, she cut away the blood-encrusted portion of his shirt, completely baring the wound. Rising, she fetched the old wooden bucket used for drinking water and set it next to her patient. She tore several strips of cloth from her petticoat and gently swabbed away the crusted blood. Hastings stirred under her ministrations and blood began to well anew from the small puckered hole in his back.

"He needs a doctor," she said, looking pleadingly at Johnson. Someone had to take charge and see that Hastings received the treatment he needed. Laurie couldn't do it. Johnson was incapable because of his injury, and Jed wasn't there. Even if the others had offered she knew it would have to be her.

"Perhaps he does, ma'am," Johnson replied. "But we ain't got a doctor, and where are we going to find one who's going to come way out here? You think we can bring a doctor out here and that he's going to keep the whereabouts of this place secret? No, ma'am, we'll work it—"

"Hush, Tucker!" Margaret screamed. "It's a risk we'll have to take. Bret has lost a lot of blood and the bullet is still in there. I don't care what risk there is, we have to get him to a doctor so that bullet can be removed—otherwise he may die. I'm sure Dr. Loring can be trusted. He'll come. You wait and see, and he won't tell about it afterward. He was a very good friend of my father's, and I think I know him well."

Johnson could see that she was determined to go despite anything he might say. It was a gamble, he knew, but just being here was a risk—so why not go along with

148

her? He wasn't even sure he could agree with her about Hastings' condition. Wounds were common enough, and this one didn't look as if it would be fatal despite the loss of blood. He decided to humor her. Women puzzled him and he was never quite sure just how to deal with them. Margaret was now struggling with a saddle. The desire to help her was there, but with his injured ankle he would be more of a bother than a help. She might interpret his lack of aid as a disconcern for Hastings. To hell with her, he thought, I don't care what she thinks. She can put all four of our necks in a noose and it won't make a damn bit of difference to me.

"Margaret, Dr. Loring isn't in town," Laurie blurted out. "He left for Kansas City early yesterday morning— for supplies, I think."

"Are you sure, Laurie? He usually sends someone or orders them sent to him."

"I know. This time he went. I saw him. He was boarding the early stage while I was eating breakfast. I saw him through the window."

"It doesn't matter," Margaret said. "Bret needs a doctor. I'll ride to the fort. Doc will come."

At that Johnson unintentionally set his injured foot down solidly and winced from the pain. "You can't do that!" he growled. "My God, woman! What do you think your husband will do? He ain't exactly pleased that you run off with a saddle tramp. No! It's out of the question!" Johnson leaned back against the cave wall and sighed.

"Doc may be a drunken sot but he's skilled," she said, ignoring Johnson. "Besides, he hasn't been drunk once since he's been at the fort. If I ask him to come, he'll find a way." She managed to heave a saddle up on the horse's back and was busy tightening the cinch.

Was there no way for him to dissuade her? She paid him no attention, despite the danger he was trying to make her aware of. Hell! She knew the danger as well as he did.

Just then Jed walked in from a scouting sortee.

"What's all this?" The old man looked from Margaret to Hastings. "Whur yuh afixin' tuh go, gal?"

"I'm going to the fort for Doc," she said.

"Hell no, yuh ain't! We ain't got no time for to fetch no doctor." Jed bent and examined Hastings' wound carefully. "Laurie, rinse out that there coffee pot and boil me 'bout half a pot of water. Margaret, rip up some of yer petticoat. I'm agonna need some bandages."

Laurie moved quickly to do the old man's bidding. Margaret hesitated. What did he have in mind? she wondered. And not knowing why she did it, she left the horse and began tearing the remnant of her ruined petticoat into strips. Jed's manner had instilled a confidence in her she hadn't known before.

"What happened to you, Slim, lose a boot?"

Johnson smiled. "Nope, but I found one."

Jed chuckled at the gambler's attempt at humor.

Margaret found herself smiling at Johnson's remark despite the seriousness of the moment. The companionship among them was back and stronger than before.

Jed went to his knees beside the prone body of Hastings. "Set aside, me gal," he directed Margaret. "I'm agonna need help. Bring that there coffee pot, gal," he said to Laurie, indicating a spot on his other side with a gnarled hand. He examined the wound tenderly. Hastings winced but said nothing.

Jed reached back and pulled his skinning knife from a greasy sheath on his hip. Reaching over he took one of the strips of cloth from Margaret and wiped the blade vigorously. Turning slightly, he dropped the knife into the pot of boiling water.

"Whur's that there whiskey, Slim?"

150

Johnson reached behind him and produced the bottle. A little over half of the amber fluid remained.

"Here you are, ole timer," he said.

Margaret sat on her heels to Jed's left, her knees almost touching Bret's head, watching carefully as the old man poured whiskey into the wound. Then he tilted the bottle to his lips and drank. Finally, he twisted Hastings' head up so he could also drink of the pain-numbing liquid. Margaret didn't question the old man's ability. What she didn't know was that Jed had dug many a bullet out of bleeding flesh. He could have told her about the time he had sat under a spruce tree in a lonesome winter world of the Bitterroots and dug a Crow arrow head out of his own thigh. There was also the time when his trapping partner, Hooknose Charley Brandt, had got his leg caught in a rusty old bear trap and Jed had amputated old Charley's leg after gangrene had rotted it beyond saving.

She didn't know these things, but she willingly accepted his ministrations. She was ready to assist him. Her only thoughts were of Bret and, at the moment, Jed could have been the most skilled surgeon in the country.

She waited patiently for Jed to continue the operation. Hastings was awake, his head resting on his right arm, his blue eyes turned toward her. He was smiling. She returned the smile—hot tears burning her eyes. If only she could reassure him—tell him that everything would be all right; but she couldn't speak. The lump in her throat had choked back all vocal sounds. She bent forward and kissed him lightly on the cheek and held his hand warmly in hers.

Jed poured boiling water from the coffee pot and held the steaming knife in his hand, ignoring the heat from the handle. The pain was evident but any pain was tempered by his caloused, weather-hardened skin. The greasy knife sheath had been placed in Hastings' mouth for him to bite

151

on. Jed made an exploratory probe of the wound with the pointed tip of his knife. Hastings clamped down hard on the piece of old leather but made no sound. Jed's leathery face was wrinkled with care. Momentarily his features softened, and a tiny smile flicked across his face. He had found the slug. Working around the bullet, using the point of his knife as a lever, he pried the slug upward.

"Gimme that there whiskey bottle," Margaret passed it to him and he took a long drink. Margaret moved to stop him, then drew back. He passed the bottle to her again and said, "Pour a little of that on muh hands. Not too much. It's all we got."

Jed worked his hands together, spreading the whiskey evenly over their surface, shook them to remove the excess and went back to probing. A final twist of his knife and he dipped his forefinger and thumb into the wound and withdrew a small hunk of lead flattened on two sides.

Margaret sighed with relief. Johnson watched, a look of disdain on his face. Laurie had retreated to the farthest corner of the cave unable to watch with so much blood flowing.

Hastings looked up at Margaret. His face was pale—a ghostly whiteness in the dim candle light, but he was still smiling.

"Is that old butcher through with me now?"

"Yes, dear," Margaret said.

"He's lucky," Jed said. "He caught that there bullet agoin' away and it was damn near spent. Twenty yards closer and we'd be aburyin' him instead of carvin' on him. It got stuck 'twixt a couple of ribs. Chipped one amight. I reckon that's what stopped it—kept it from goin' any deeper. As it is it didn't much more'n make a hole in his hide." He swabbed away the oozing blood with one of the strips of petticoat. Then he folded a clean strip of cloth into a square compress and placed it over the wound.

After soaking it liberally with whiskey, he secured it in place by binding several more strips around Hastings' torso and over his shoulder. It had the look of a professional job.

"That orta hold him," Jed said. He went over and examined Johnson's ankle. "Better keep that propped up some. I'll bind it afore we leave."

"Leave!" Johnson exploded. "Where the hell are we goin'?"

"Ain't sure, yet," Jed said. "Camp Robinson more'n likely. We cain't stay here nohow. Them there hills is lousy with brown uniforms, and it'll only be a matter of time 'till they find this here place. I aim tuh git the jump on 'em. They'll most likely settle down some tonight. So as soon as it gets dark we pull out. They ain't likely tuh see us scamperin' outa there in the dark, so everybody git some sleep. Yuh might not git another chance fer a spell."

15

Margaret awoke. The sputtering candles were down to their last light, and she hurriedly lit fresh ones that Jed had brought from town. Jed was gone, but the others were still sleeping. She checked Hastings. His breathing was regular and there was more color in his cheeks. She brushed a shock of brown hair out of his eyes and returned to her chores.

In a matter of minutes Jed returned. "Howdy, gal," he said. "Them there soldier-boys is camped down stream aways. Looks like a good time to skedaddle."

Jed busied himself saddling the horses while Margaret prepared a meager breakfast. After their meal Jed bound Johnson's ankle. Johnson managed to clamber into the saddle unassisted. Hastings, sitting up and sipping scalding coffee, looked more alive than he had earlier in the day after Jed's improvised operation. He kept eyeing his horse and would have tried to mount, but Jed brought out an Indian-style travois which he must have fashioned while the others slept. At first, Hastings refused to ride in "that contraption" as he called it. Jed was adamant and, finally, Hastings relented and lay down on the travois after Jed has fastened it securely to the horse. Margaret tucked blankets around him, kissed him quickly on the lips, and prepared herself to leave.

They rode slowly through the long night. At Hastings' insistence Margaret wore his mackinaw to protect her from the chill night air. Jed said there was a smell of snow in the air but the sky was clear. They rode on through the next day, tiring the horses and wearying themselves. As the sun settled on the horizon, Jed called a halt.

He led them into a sheltered place at the foot of a nearby butte. An eroded gully, a dozen feet wide, had been carved in the talus at the lower edge of the butte. A shelf made of more resistant rock than that above and below it provided a roof of sorts along one side. Weird-shaped rocks weathered by the wind lay on the other sides, thus enclosing the small area on all sides except for the trail they had followed in.

Jed, as fresh as when they had started, unsaddled the horses and built a roaring fire. Hastings questioned the wisdom of a fire since it could pinpoint their position if they were being followed. Jed shrugged it off, saying something about being more worried about the cold than he was about any pursuers.

After supper Jed rolled up his blankets and was snoring almost immediately. Laurie retreated as far from the others as she dared and made up her bed and settled in. Hastings, who had been sitting near the fire since before supper, now appeared to be asleep, rolled up in his blankets. The fire had died to a mass of glowing-red coals with a tiny flame sputtering to life briefly every so often to consume a tiny bit of unburned wood. Margaret sat on a flat-topped rock, her hands spread toward the fire. She still wore Hastings' mackinaw and, in addition, had draped a blanket over her shoulders. Tucker Johnson was off to one side of the fire, his legs stretched out before him with his back and elbows resting against a log, a cigar clamped tightly in his teeth.

Margaret surveyed the lanky gambler, and some of the

strangeness of him that had troubled Hastings now occupied her mind. After a long period of silence she said, "Tucker, you're a puzzling man. You're not at all what you seem to be."

Johnson glanced at her suspiciously as he removed the cigar from his mouth, then shot a quick glance at Hastings, before turning back to her.

"Is that a fact, ma'am," he said after a while.

"What are you hiding? Won't you tell me about it?"

"I don't know what you mean, ma'am." He looked a bit uneasy.

"Most of the time you're just putting on an act. You try to appear apathetic and stupid, but you're really very clever and intelligent. Why do you do these things?"

"Well, ma'am, I ain't never told anyone about me. It's because—because I'm scared, I reckon," he said meekly.

"You, afraid? That's hard to believe."

"It's true, ma'am. The act—well, it gives me the courage I need to survive in this life I've chosen for myself. It's the same with Bret-boy here," he said, pointing at Hastings. "He don't give a damn whether he lives or dies so he stays calm—though he ain't as calm anymore as he once was, and I reckon I know why. Me, I want to stay alive, so I let the other feller think I ain't so bright and about half asleep. That makes him feel confident, then at the last minute I let him see I ain't what he thinks I am. It tends to confuse him a might, but mostly it relaxes me, I reckon. Speed may be important but it ain't so significant as steady nerves. If you stay calm, you win. Only one feller I ever saw could stay as cool as Bret-boy in a gunfight and that was Doc Holliday. In some ways Doc's like Bret-boy. Ole Doc's nerves stem from the fact that he's dyin' from consumption anyway."

She had suspected something of the sort about Bret and she had wondered about Tucker. She was eager to hear more about him, and he seemed to be in an unusually talkative mood tonight.

"You weren't always a gambler were you, Tucker?" She moved closer to the fire, stirring the coals and adding another chunk of wood.

"No, ma'am," Johnson replied, watching the tongues of yellow flame lick up along the sides of the wood. He tossed his dead cigar into the flames, settled back more comfortably against the log and launched into his story.

"My pa was a preacherman—leastwise he was on Sunday. I never knew my ma. She died when I was born. We lived on a little farm back in Indiana. Pa was a big gruff man. He was always preachin' hell-fire and damnation at me, and what he couldn't preach into me he tried to beat into me with a stout hickory rod. So, naturally, ever chance I got I did as many of the things he told me not to as I could." He smiled.

"We never got along. I reckon it was because I never understood him, and he couldn't understand me neither. The day after I turned sixteen I ran off and joined the army. I got in just at the tailend of the big war. I saw some action, not much to speak of, but in general I liked army life. I guess that's where I learned to gamble, and it didn't take me long to learn that I was good at poker. A natural instinct, I reckon. That's when I started the sleepyeyed act. It worked real nice for bluffin'." He dug out another cigar and lit it with a glowing twig from the fire.

"After the war I went west. I had decided to stay in the army awhile longer. I was assigned to the Seventh Cavalry. I was with Custer at both of his big fights. In sixty-eight down on the Washita we wiped out a bunch of Cheyenne under ole Black Kettle. That battle didn't bother me none 'cause we was gettin' the best of it—except for Major Elliott's detachment—the whole time. The other fight, up on the Little Big Horn, was

157

different. We got the worst of it that time. Lucky for me, I reckon, that ole Longhair split the regiment into three groups. I was with Reno and I thought for a while there ole Chief Gall and his Hunkpapa Sioux was going to do for us. We made a run for the bluffs along the river and holed up there for a while to fight." He shuddered as the memory of the battle washed over him. Margaret felt his uneasiness, and she couldn't look at him but instead stared into the fire.

"Ole Gall gave us fits for a while. Then somthin' prompted him to leave us and ride off. We learned later that him and Crazy Horse had caught Custer up on that hill." He trembled as he relit his cigar. After the cigar was going well he went on with his story.

He talked of the fighting and waiting that made up the next couple of days. He told how they had found Custer's five troops of cavalry, scalped, naked, and mutilated; and about the burying that followed. "That was it, I didn't want no more of the army. As soon as my hitch was up, I got out. There wasn't much I knew how to do 'cept ride a horse, shoot a gun, and play cards, so I decided bein' a gambler was as good a way for me as any. I was good at it, and it had a certain glamor and adventure, and I could be as lazy as I wanted to be. I soon found out, though, that if a gambler wants to go on livin', he's got to know how to use a pistol. I did, and with the act I contrived for myself, I did right well. I hired out my gun on occasion but mostly I stuck to gamblin'."

"What the hell you doin' here, then?" Hastings was sitting up in his blankets.

Johnson reddened, embarrassed that Hastings had overheard. "I reckon I ain't told you everything about this job."

"Why not tell us about it then?" Hastings asked sarcastically, edging closer to the fire.

"I had every intention of tellin' you before long." He paused, then went on. "Part of it was Slater's money, but mostly it was bigger stakes."

"Bigger stakes? Such as?" Hastings asked.

"Silver, Bret-boy, silver. That's where you come in, Miss Margaret."

Hastings and Margaret exchanged puzzled looks.

"Forgive me, ma'am, but you are the main reason I bought in with Bret-boy here. I knew he was close to you."

None of it made any sense to her, and she certainly was bewildered by her part in it. She had noticed that he had said the main reason was silver. His other reason had to be Bret. Johnson was clever but he hadn't been able to hide his affection for Bret from her. His statement now confirmed what she had thought all along.

"Whoa, boy," Hastings said. "You'd better start from the beginning. You lost me back there aways."

Johnson nodded and drew on his cigar. "It was several years ago in Kansas City. Slater had a place there. I used to play cards there some."

"You knew Slater before?" Hastings asked.

"Only to look at. We never met. He might have seen me playin' cards in his place, but not so he remembered me anyhow." He stopped to puff on his cigar and shifted his position slightly.

Hastings and Margaret remained silent, listening intently.

"Gamblin' in a place a feller learns a lot about what's goin' on if he keeps his ears open. Seems an old fellow was comin' into town ever couple of months with a silver poke he was cashin' in. Slater learned about it and found out that the old man was comin' in from out here— Northgate. About that time I moseyed on to Dodge City. Then, awhile ago I heard Slater's lookin' for a gun and he's out here now where the silver was comin' from. I figger Slater is on to somethin'—so I aimed to cut myself in."

Margaret was the only one aware that he was mixing his act with his real self and had been doing so for the whole evening. The more excited or angry he was, she saw the more he was his real self.

"What's all this to do with Margaret?" Hastings asked.

"The old man with the silver poke was her father."

"Daddy had silver! I never knew a thing about it."

"I figured you didn't, but not until I had sided with this yahoo. Now Bret-boy, I'll fill you in on the rest you don't know. It took me a time to learn it all, but it fits in. That night at old man Taylor's shack—excuse me, ma'am—when Taylor was shot by Henry with my rifle."

"Yeah. What about it?" Hastings asked.

"Henry didn't miss. Ike Henry never missed what he shot at. Maybe he was a drunk and a noaccount but he could shoot a rifle. He was a sharp shooter in the army. No, sir, Henry shot Taylor and it was Taylor he was paid to shoot. At first I thought you were the target, Bret-boy, just like you did. Then, like I told you, I found out it was Slater that snuck my rifle. He wanted a scapegoat in case Denton got wise, and you, Bret-boy, spoiled his plans somewhat."

"But why did he shoot Taylor? Slater didn't find the silver did he?"

"Nope. Nobody's found it yet. Slater figured Denton knew about the silver too. As Slater saw it, that's why Denton married you, Miss Margaret. He thought Denton must be gettin' close to findin' out about the whereabouts of the silver, that's why he had your father killed. Slater figured with him out of the way it evened his chances with Denton in findin' the silver."

"But if there is any silver, I'm sure John knows nothing of it," Margaret said.

160

"That's the way I see it too," Johnson said.

"How does Norwood fit into this with Slater?" Hastings asked.

"Him and Norwood owned that saloon jointly in Kansas City. They worked the whole deal out together on a fifty-fifty basis. Norwood was a big cattle man down in Texas, and he supplied most of the money for the place out here. Slater's part of the deal was to be here, run the saloon, and try to find the silver. Norwood got impatient with Slater when he heard about Taylor's death and he rushed up here, pronto. By this time Slater had come to realize he had made a mistake in killin' Taylor and had found out that Denton was just plain loco and didn't give a damn about any silver."

"But it was too late then. Margaret was their only chance but they didn't know how to get her away from Denton without settin' him and his entire army after them, so they were just playin' along until a chance for them came up. It was only a coincidence that you happened to be here, Bret-boy. Apparently, Norwood finally accepted what Slater had done. Now, when Denton makes his move, they plan to move in. They can't fight him. He's too strong."

"Incredible!" Hastings said.

"Hey, yuh three agonna go on ajawin' all night? Get some sleep—we got a long ride ahead of us tommory," Jed grumbled as he turned over in his blankets.

Johnson smiled sheepishly. "I reckon I'll turn in; I'm all tuckered out." He yawned and stretched.

Hastings lay down, and Margaret snuggled down into her bed of blankets near the fire. In time silence reigned except for an assortment of raucus snores and the far-off howling of a lone wolf.

16

As the first gray-pink streaks of dawn broke the horizon,
Jed rolled out of his bankets and made up his bedroll. He
was feeling the exhilaration of the old days when camp
fires were many and rising in the cold, crisp, first light of
morning was a daily experience. He stirred the fire but
found nothing other than gray ashes. Hesitating momentarily he considered building the fire anew, then discarded
the idea. Astride his mount he urged the animal out of
camp at a walk for a hundred yards, then spurred it into a
fast trot, heading in a northeasterly direction.

Minutes after Jed's departure, Hastings awoke. His
shoulder was stiff and ached with a subdued constant
pain. He felt much stronger and managed to get to his
feet. Jed's absence was immediately obvious, but it didn't
overly concern him, and he set about building a fire and
getting the coffee on. The wind lashed briskly through the
camp, and he shivered with the cutting chill as he looked
out across the prairie.

Margaret sat up sleepy-eyed, trying to knuckle away
the cobwebs of somnolence from her eyes. Seeing Bret up
and around, she hurried to his side to take over the
breakfast preparations, scolding him for being on his feet
so soon and for not waking her. After all he was not a well

man, and the camp chores should be left to her and the others. He smiled at her apologetically. She gradually cajoled him into sitting on the log Johnson had used for a backrest the night before while she finished breakfast.

The heat of the roaring fire drifted over the supine form of Johnson. The sudden change in temperature roused him and he sat up, surly at being awakened before his customary time. There was no one paying him enough attention on whom he could vent his anger, so it subsided quickly. Rising, he tested his injured ankle and found that he could support his weight on it for short periods without excessive pain. For that he felt gratified—having to depend on others didn't set right with him. He took a seat on the log beside Hastings and stretched his feet out toward the fire.

Laurie was the last to rise. She came over to the fireside quietly, brushing her tangled hair into place with her hands. She did not speak to anyone, but accepted her plate and withdrew to her place away from them where she ate in silence.

The sky had darkened to a leaden-gray overnight, and the first large flakes of snow of Jed's promised storm drifted silently over their camp. The wind was quickening with strong gusts, whipping snow around them and bending the flames of the fire. They huddled closer to the warmth, drawing woolen blankets about them to dispel the cold.

During one of the wind lulls, Hastings spied a dark speck flitting along the far southeastern horizon. Then just as quickly the image was erased from view by the swirling snow, swept along by the roaring wind.

"Someone's comin'!" he shouted over the wind. "I seen a rider off to the southeast there," he called, extending his arm from beneath the blanket. They all looked in the direction he had indicated, but the raging

163

storm blotted everything from view except the features near the camp. Hastings lifted his pistol gently out of his holster and settled it back into place lightly. Johnson, a blanket draped loosely over his shoulders, drew his pistol, held it up, spun the cylinder and checked the loads. Margaret, shivering, stretched out a booted toe and pushed a partially-charred bit of wood further into the fire. She glanced once more toward the southeast, then moved closer to Bret, sought his arm and clung possessively to him. Hastings raised his right arm and clasped her around the shoulders, drawing her in close to him.

They heard the plodding sound of hooves striking solid ground intermittently over the noise of the storm, but they could still see nothing but wind-whipped snow. Then, like an apparition from nowhere, Jed appeared, riding in out of the driving snowstorm.

"How on earth did you find us in this?" Margaret asked, gesturing at the storm, and feeling relief in knowing that the rider was Jed.

Jed didn't answer but dismounted and crowded in close to the fire, extending his gnarled, wrinkled hands. Looking directly at Hastings, he said, "They're out thar. Fifteen, mebbe twenty of 'em. They ain't but three, four hours ride away. I didn't get that close a look but I reckon they're afollowin' the valley. I could see 'em from the top of that there mesa over lookin' chimney rock. Then this dadgummed storm blew up, and I couldn't see a blasted thing!"

"Is Beau with them?" Laurie asked anxiously.

"Cain't rightly say. I didn't get near enough tuh make out no faces, but them there brown unee-forms is clear at quite a distance."

"What do we do now?" Margaret asked.

"How fast are they moving?" Johnson put in.

164

The old man looked around at the circle of expectant faces, dug a plug of tobacco from his vest pocket and sliced off a chunk. "They'll be on us afore dark." He tucked the piece of tobacco into his cheek, and his jaws worked furiously.

"I don't see how they can catch up to us if we keep moving," Margaret said, brushing a strand of stray hair out of her eyes. "Especially in this storm. Surely, they won't be able to find us in this snowstorm."

Jed spat a stream of dark-brown liquid into the fire and listened to it sizzle. Shifting the cud to his other cheek, he said, "This here storm ain't agonna last." Then as if reacting to his words, the wind began to die. The swirling snow began to settle and the sun peeked through the hazy overcast.

"And besides," Jed continued, "as near as I could tell, each of them there soldier-boys has got two horses. That means they can travel a damn sight faster'n a whole lot further then we can!"

After the report from Jed, Hastings knew they had no chance to outrun their pursuers. With the white mantle of snow covering everything, they couldn't throw the army off their trail. They could only run until caught or stand and fight.

Jed's intentions were clear, and he had already begun to clear the camp and to saddle horses. The wind, so strong before, had now subsided to a brisk breeze, and only a few ragged clouds hung on as evidence of the storm. The snow was shallow but, in places, the wind had swept the prairie floor clear of snow only to drift it in another.

Hastings was thinking of the plight of the girls. There was no need for them to be taken. He glanced over at Johnson who was seated on the log before the waning fire. Johnson caught his look and returned a hooded wink.

Tuck knew what he was thinking and he was anxious for it to begin.

"Jed, wait!" Hastings said as he walked toward the old man who stood adjusting a stirrup. Bannock turned to face him as he approached.

"What is it, young feller?" he asked.

"You ride on to Camp Robinson with the women, talk to the commandant and see if he won't send cavalry out here to help. In any case, make sure that the girls are safe. This place is well protected, and Tuck and me can hold them off for quite a spell—long enough for you to get some troops back here to help."

"The hell yuh say! I ain't ridin' off and leavin' you two yahoos tuh do all the fightin'. Hell, boy this here is the mostest fun I've had in a coon's age! I ain't about tuh go escortin' them there gals out of here! They can go to Camp Robinson themselves and tell that there colonel what kind of a fix we is in."

"No, they can't!" Hastings retorted, his voice fuming with anger. The old man had to see it his way. "They don't know the way and besides, you would only get in the way here."

"Why, yuh young whelp! I orta—"

"That's enough now! Get on that horse and ride. You getting the soldiers is our only chance. You have to convince the commandant there that his assistance is desperately needed to stop Denton. Now get! Don't waste any more time. You need as much of a start as you can get."

Grumbling, Jed acquiesced, and stood by like a whipped dog while Hastings outlined his plan to the others. After Jed and the girls were on their way, Hastings and Johnson positioned themselves at strategic points behind rocks, rifles ready.

Johnson lit his last cigar and puffed idly. "Thanks for

volunteerin' my services, Bret-boy. Just what I needed—a gunfight with Denton's soldierboys. What are you aimin' to do after we whip 'em?"

Hastings grinned at Johnson's remark. Tuck knew as well as he did that neither of them would leave this place alive, and it was only a matter of time until the soldiers closed in on them. His only hope was that they could delay long enough for Jed and the girls to reach the safety of Camp Robinson. There wasn't time for any help to return. Denton's Army would overrun them long before any help could arrive. Meanwhile, he and Tuck would take as many of Denton's Army with them as they could.

"I hope that bastard is ridin' out in the lead," Hastings muttered.

"What'd you say, Bret-boy?" Johnson asked.

"Nothin'," Hastings said.

The hours dragged. Muscles grew tired and stiff from lack of movement, and eyes were strained by staring into the glaring whiteness hour after hour. The sun, now unobstructed by clouds, quickly warmed the air, and they felt comfortable. Finally, they saw them coming in columns of two, Hardian and Burton sharing the lead. There was no sign of Denton.

"This is it," said Hastings with a sigh of relief. "I'm sure glad to have got to know you, Tuck. When this is over, the man who has the shortest tally of brown-suited soldierboys buys the whiskey."

"You're on. Hope you got a pocket full of coins, 'cause when this is over I'm gonna have a powerful thirst."

"It'll be you what's buying," Hastings said. "You won't be able to stay awake long enough to get more'n two or three."

The lanky gambler laughed and sighting along his rifle, he drew a bead on one of the nearer riders as the columns turned broadside to them, executing a turn. Johnson

167

squeezed the trigger, and the fancy buffalo gun roared across the prairie. A soldier pitched from his saddle. Hastings' first shot followed close behind, and before the first man hit the ground, another saddle was emptied.

A moment of chaos among the troops came and passed as their trained instincts took over and they rode out of range to reconnoiter.

"Did you get a count, Tuck?" Hastings called.

"Nope. Figured you'd do that. Anyhow we each got one that time," Johnson replied.

"Well, let's figure there was twenty of 'em. That means we got eighteen to go. Here they come again!"

They came at a full gallop, spread out, offering only small targets to the besieged gunmen in the rocks. Johnson and Hastings, unrattled, took careful aim and fired together. Two riders jerked in their saddles and fell to the ground, and the riderless horses plunged on out of danger. Hastings swung his rifle around and snapped off a quick shot at a rider coming his way. A miss! The riders came on; then, on cue, they reared their horses and slid to the ground. The waist-high grass hid them effectively despite the snow. A damn good move! Hastings thought as he mentally tallied the troops. Ten, and he and Johnson had accounted for two of them before they had completed their maneuver. There was still eight or maybe ten more camped back out of range. What was their next move going to be?

The eight in the grass were holding their attention. Part of the group would rise and fire, drawing return shots. Obviously, others in the grass were edging closer to their fortress. For an hour the battle waged with neither side scoring a hit. Hastings and Johnson had kept the soldiers' progress slow but they hadn't been able to completely stop them from getting closer to their position.

A lull in the shooting came. The two men looked

carefully to see what had happened to cause the siege to diminish. A moment passed. A false hope rose. The fusillade began anew at greatly increased frequency and intensity. A shadow fell across Johnson's broad back, and he swung around, facing the south end of their redoubt. There atop one of the wind-shaped rocks stood Beau Hardian!

Hardian dropped lightly into the small enclosure, still facing Johnson. Hastings, unaware of Hardian's presence within their fortress, continued to fire at the advancing troops.

"Drop your guns, Johnson! It's all over now. There's no sense in resisting. You'll die anyway," Hardian announced.

Johnson threw his now empty rifle to the ground and backed away from Hardian toward Hastings' position, his right hand hovering over his holstered gunbutt. Hastings, partially deafened by the noise of exploding shells, did not hear the exchange between Johnson and Hardian.

"That's far enough, big man. One more step and I'll shoot!" Johnson rasped.

"Haa!" Hardian exploded. "I don't think you'll shoot an unarmed man and I carry no weapon. See!" Hardian continued toward Johnson, his stone-chiseled face free of emotion.

What in hell is wrong with this man's thinking? Johnson wondered. Does he really think I won't shoot him just because he's unarmed? Hardian drew closer. Johnson's hand blurred, and a finger squeezed the trigger. The force of the bullet stopped the big man in mid-stride—yet Hardian smiled, ignoring the pain as blood darkened the front of his shirt, and he kept advancing toward Johnson.

Johnson moved back desperately and came up against

a rock. Retreat could go no further. Panic rose, and he fired again and again, snapping off shots in rapid succession. Each bullet hit its mark and caused the big man to falter, but only for an instant, then on he came. Johnson fumbled for fresh shells, but there was no time to reload. Hardian was on him now! He searched frantically for a weapon, then threw up his hands to ward off Hardian's attack. It was useless. Even with six bullets in his chest, Hardian's strength was superior.

Hastings, busy with the men slowly advancing in the grass, was unaware of what was happening to Johnson, until he glanced in Johnson's direction in time to see Hardian with his face turned skyward, his shirtfront soaked red with blood, his massive hands gripping Tucker Johnson's throat with superhuman strength. Streams of sweat trickled down Hardian's face despite the biting chill of the air. Johnson's face was turning a dark bluish-purple, his eyes were bulging and his thickening tongue was thrust out between swollen lips. Hastings took careful aim and fired. Hardian's head snapped back jerkily. A small red hole appeared in Hardian's forehead, and an expression of utmost surprise covered his face. Gradually, his grip loosened and Johnson fell limply to the ground. Hardian staggered back a step—two steps, then he pitched forward and fell on his face.

"Hastings!" A voice called from behind him. He turned around. There stood Nick Burton, a leer on his face, his guns leveled. Hastings dropped his gun and slowly raised his hands. It had been the first time for him to face Denton's little gunfighter. Burton's face was screwed into a perpetual frown. The baggy uniform added to his appearance of slenderness. Even so, his eyes formed wide slits in his ugly face, and his gunhands were steady with confidence.

"They tell me you're quite handy with a pistol," the

little man sneered. "You want to try and see just how fast you are? I'll wager with an even start I could drop you before you got your gun free of your holster."

Hastings considered the challenge. Was the little man actually going to give him a chance? It wouldn't make a difference. They would kill him eventually anyway. Why not take the challenge? Maybe, at least, he could kill Burton. He started to bend over to retrieve his fallen pistol.

"It's over, Hastings! Don't pick it up! Captain Denton wants to see you!" The voice was firm and rang with authority.

He recognized the grizzled old sergeant Margaret had been so fond of. The other troopers were gathering around now, and each held a gun trained on him. Burton's eyes were fixed on him, a challenging leer on his face.

17

The ride to Denton's fort was a long, slow journey. All
around him rode the brown-clad troopers of Denton's
army. These men seemed to be of one type—cast from the
same mold, hard of feature and cruel of nature. They were
men with no compassion—men who served a merciless
master to whom each was blindly obedient.

As the entourage approached the fort, Hastings
surveyed the structure. The outside consisted of a solid
wall of vertical logs, most of them pointed at the top. The
main gate, composed of two split-log doors, swung open
to meet them. Inside, a quick perusal registered the
impregnable nature of the fortress and its simplicity.
Barracks, mess hall, and other quarters for the troopers
formed the end walls. For the most part they were
one-story edifices, giving an appearance of one long
building with many doors. Where no buildings stood, tall
pointed palisades stripped of bark denied access to
anyone approaching from the outside. To the left of the
main gate was the parade ground, worn bare by the
endless tread of marching feet and stamping hooves. To
the right was Denton's house, a two-story structure which
did not form any part of the fort's outer wall. Running
along the front and side of the house visible to him was a

wide veranda. Above the roof of the veranda, around the eaves, was a narrow widow's walk from which the commanding officer might view his men at all points within the enclosure.

He did not have long to familiarize himself with the fort's interior because once inside the gate he was hustled into a small room within the barracks complex in a rear corner beyond the parade ground. This small room proved to be the guard house—a small cell constructed completely of logs tightly chinked together. The back wall consisted of the outer palisades, the poles of which extended well above the roof of the structure. The side walls were composed of logs laid horizontally and formed a common wall with the adjacent barracks. The front of the cell was also built of horizontal logs, fitted with a large door, fashioned of rough-hewn timbers. A small, square hole just large enough for a man to put his head through was cut in the topcenter of the door. Inside the cell he found that this window was the only source of light, creating a dusky murkiness in the tiny room.

As his eyes became accustomed to the darkness, he sensed the presence of another besides himself in the tiny cell. Daylight was waning but the identity of his cellmate was evident.

"Slater! How did you get here?" This was novel, finding Slater here! He should have anticipated something of the sort.

Slater scowled at him. "I've been trying to figure that out for myself." Slater was in a prone position on a small bed on the hard-packed earth of the cell floor, with his hands laced together behind his head.

"Where's Norwood?" Hastings asked. "Still runnin' around loose? Seems Denton would want to keep the two of you together." His dislike for the man was mounting. It was like sharing quarters with an animal with a malodorous stench.

173

"Haa!" Slater snorted. "Norwood's dead. You killed him and two of our men in that shootout you had behind my place the other night. You and that ingrate, Johnson." Slater's bitterness showed with the curl of his lip in the semi-darkness.

"I didn't know," Hastings admitted as he eased his lanky frame down onto the thin, straw-filled canvas pallet across from Slater. "We knew we had hit someone—more than one, really—but it was so dark we had no way of knowing who it was. He brought it upon himself."

"It doesn't matter now," Slater said bitterly. "We're both at the mercy of this fiend, Denton. You ... you've got plenty of reason for being here. Me, I tried to help him, and this is what I get!" Slater said disgustedly. He got to his feet and moved to the door to peer out into the gathering gloom as if he might find help in the courtyard.

"Norwood's last man followed you that night. By the way, where is Johnson?" he asked as he suddenly spun around to look at Hastings.

"He's dead," Hastings replied simply.

"Serves him right!" Slater snapped as he lay back down on his pallet, trying to find some degree of comfort on the rock-hard, dirt floor. "Norwood's man marked your cave well, then reported to me. I paid him and came out here. I knew Denton was looking for you and Johnson, so I figured he would appreciate the information. He seemed appreciative at first all right, then he changed all at once. It was like he resented what I had found out and was furious that it came from me rather than from his own men. After I had finished telling him what I knew, he ordered his men to throw me in here. It was right then that I told him in no uncertain terms just what I thought of him! I felt sure he was going to explode. He got redder than the sun at sundown." Slater chuckled to himself, then lapsed off into silence.

174

Hastings was uncomfortable on the hard ground. His wounds ached, and he felt weak and exhausted. Despite the discomfort, he welcomed the chance to relax. After considerable shifting around, he settled down and drifted off to sleep. Much later he awoke. The sky was stained with the first pink light of dawn. Immediately, he sensed something different—something he couldn't identify—a certain indefinite uneasiness which usually ended up in trouble. He glanced over at Slater. The saloon keeper was motionless, and his even breathing indicated he was still asleep.

The click of a key turning in the lock broke the stillness. Hastings got to his feet painfully and backed away from the door as it swung open. Standing there, framed by the doorway, was a man, spare of build with a rapidly receding hairline, and dressed in the familiar dark-brown uniform with corporal's stripes on the sleeves. Beyond him stood two more soldiers, each holding a rifle with bayonets fixed.

"Slater!" the corporal barked loudly.

Slater fought his way up out of his trance-like sleep. "W . . . w . . . what is it?" he muttered.

"You. Come with me," the corporal barked in a strained monotone.

"Why?" Slater asked, trying to bolster his courage.

"No questions!" the corporal barked. "Now, move before I lose my temper altogether!"

Hastings watched him go. A guard detail escorted him across the parade ground toward the house, and the last he saw of Slater was an armed escort at each elbow, marching him toward the house with the spritely corporal leading the way.

The guard outside the cell relocked the door, and Hastings was left alone with his thoughts. He returned to his pallet.

He had slept well despite the hardships. Now the gnawing ache in his shoulder, together with the biting rawness of the chill air made it difficult for him to doze off to sleep again. Restlessness plagued him, and he shifted his weight almost constantly only to find that his body experienced another bothersome pain. A half-hour passed, and he still found sleep elusive—then the echoing reports of several rifles rent the still air. Hastings leapt to his feet, ignoring the shooting pain, and dashed to the door to look outside. All he could see was the bored guard outside the cell door drawing designs in the dirt with his booted toe.

"What were those shots?" he asked.

"Those came from the firing squad over on the t'other side of the house. Slater sure won't cuss the old man anymore." He chuckled. "No, sir! Cap'n Denton don't take no back talk off nobody. I reckon you'll get yours directly."

Hastings said nothing and returned to his pallet. He had to find a way out of here, and it wouldn't be easy. The cell was well constructed. If Denton had Slater shot for cussing him, what would he do to him who had killed a number of his men—and had stolen his wife? How long would Denton wait? Dare he hope that Jed could reach Camp Robinson in time to bring help?

As the minutes ticked by, he lost himself so deeply in thought that he failed to hear the key turning in the lock, and when the door swung open it startled him. Even more of a shock was the figure he encountered in the doorway. He rose to his feet slowly. The shock of seeing Margaret standing there before him with a tray of food on her arm was almost more than he could stand. It was not the same Margaret he had said goodbye to the previous morning. This Margaret was a ghastly sight. Her face was a grotesque, swollen mass of greenish-blue bruises. One eye was swollen completely shut and looked like a bloodless cut beneath a sandy eyebrow.

"Margaret!" he gasped.

"I'm not very pretty to look at," she said brokenly. "I brought you some breakfast." He took the tray and looked with speechless anguish at the damage done to her.

After he had accepted the tray, Margaret stepped on through the door and stood before him. The guard locked the door, leaving her alone with him. He took her hands and drew her down beside him on the straw pallet. "John did this?" he asked, knowing the answer before he formed the question.

"Yes," she replied. She hung her head, staring at the mat between them as if she were ashamed of her present appearance.

"It's the worst beating he has ever given me. It was horrible, Bret!" she sobbed brokenly. "He used his fists and a riding crop!" She paused to look into his face with her one good eye. "Don't worry though, it's not as bad as it appears. There are no bones broken—only these bruises. I'll look hideous for a few days, but I'll be all right. It isn't permanent."

"But why... how... how did you get here?" He was puzzled. She should have been at Camp Robinson—not here amongst Denton's army.

"That's a long story," she said. "Yesterday, after we left you and Tucker, we rode toward Camp Robinson. Jed was anxious to get there—for that matter, we all were. We didn't know how long you and Tucker could hold out back there among those rocks." She shifted her position slightly, tucking her skirt tightly around her legs.

"We rode on for almost an hour. I was riding beside Laurie, and Jed was a few yards ahead, leading the way. Laurie was very quiet." She paused to touch her swollen face lightly as if to make certain it was still disfigured. The guard outside was singing softly to himself, and the haunting melody drifted through the window, lending to the nostalgia of the moment.

"Laurie didn't have much to say; then all of a sudden she began to talk about Beau. You know, Bret, she's crazy in love with him. I didn't know what to say to her." She reached up and brushed a stray wisp of hair back into place. "Now, I know Beau, and the opinion I have of him—the image I see—is just not the same as she sees him. She kept saying things about him being back there with you and how he might be in danger. She was sure that you or Tucker would kill him, and that he wouldn't have a chance because he didn't carry a gun. I just didn't know what to say."

"She's partly right," Hastings said. "He didn't have a gun and the damn fool challenged Tuck. Tuck shot him six times and it didn't stop him. I never seen anything like it. He just kept comin' until he got his hands around Tuck's throat, then he just squeezed the life out of him. I don't know what the man could have been thinking. He certainly didn't know Tucker Johnson." Hastings shook his head in disbelief. "I saw what was goin' on but not in time to save Tuck. Damnit! I shot Hardian in the head. That did for him."

"Oh, it's so horrible, Bret! Why does there have to be so much bloodshed? I suppose John's at fault. If it hadn't been for him, all those people would still be alive."

Hastings twisted the end of his mustache. "We can't tag the whole blame on John. I reckon Slater, Norwood, Tuck, and me—especially me—has to carry some of the blame. But that don't tell me how Johnson got his hands on you."

"You'd better eat your breakfast," she urged. "It's getting cold."

He looked at the food and began to eat.

"Laurie said something about having to go back and find Beau; said she just had to be with him. So she turned her horse around and headed back toward that camp just as fast as her horse could run." The tip of her tongue skipped lightly over her swollen puffed lips. He noticed that her teeth were intact. Denton had had the foresight not to permanently ruin her beauty. That fact stirred a flicker of hope deep within him. It might be possible that Denton had punished her as much as he was going to, and that he would let her live.

"I called after her, but she either didn't hear me or chose to ignore me. I don't know which. I called Jed, and he came back to where I had stopped and watched as she drew away from us. He sat there in the saddle for a moment, then gave me directions and told me to ride on alone, that he was going after Laurie." She paused to clear her throat, swallowing with noticeable difficulty. "You know how obligated he feels toward her. That's the last I saw of them. I don't know what happened to them nor where they might be now."

Wrinkles of worry were apparent around her eyes.

"I rode on like Jed told me to do. I got to the point where the trail went between two mesas." She paused and looked at him to see if he might know the place she spoke of. "It was sort of a broad valley, separating the two highlands. It was just past there that I ran into John and a dozen of his men. Apparently he had planned to catch us from each side; to meet Hardian, with us in the middle—or so I thought at the time. I didn't know what to expect from him next. I could see he was angry because his face was scarlet with rage. He just sat there on his horse and looked at me for ever so long. Finally, he asked where the rest of you were, and I just pointed and said, "Back there."

"He thought it over for a minute or two, then assigned

179

two men to ride with me before he turned his troop back toward home. I suppose he thought Beau and Nick could handle it. When we got back here he locked me in my room and let me worry about what he was going to do. I should have expected that. Much later he came to my room. He was calm and talked quite civilly, but his anger was growing again as he talked, and he went into one of his raving tantrums. That's when he beat me."

"Damn him!" Hastings muttered. A moment of silence ensued while his rage cooled, then he said, "How did you ever get him to let you come out here to see me?"

"That was his idea. I didn't even know they had taken you until this morning." She moistened her lips. "He came to my room and ordered me to fix breakfast for him and Nick. While we ate, Slater was shot. I got upset, but John just smiled and told me that you were in the guardhouse and that he wanted me to take breakfast to you and not to be concerned with Slater. So here I am." She struggled to retain her composure.

"I think he just wanted you to see me like this." She threw her hands out in a helpless gesture. "His intent, I think, is to torment you and me as much as possible. I feel certain he's going to kill us eventually. His pride won't let him do otherwise. He just wants to drag it out as long as he can."

Hastings stood, his breakfast finished, and began to pace the floor. Margaret watched him, concern showing in her eyes.

The cell door opened, and the corporal stood just outside the threshold.

"Miz Denton, your time's up. You'll accompany me back to the house." He stood back, waiting for her.

Margaret rose and daintily brushed off her skirts. She started toward the door, hesitated, turned, and came back to Hastings. She looked up into his eyes and whispered softly, "I found this," and pushed a bulky folded paper into his hand. He slipped it under his gunbelt quickly.

After she was gone, he sat unmoving for a full five minutes, giving the guard time to settle back into his languid stupor. He withdrew the paper from beneath his gunbelt and unfolded it. It was a map—a map of a battle plan. The area the map portrayed was obvious. The various arrows on the map had to represent alternate routes of attack. There was a date together with a short note scrawled hastily across the top. John Denton was planning to ride against the town and he planned to do it tomorrow! Less than twenty-four hours remained for him to get out and warn the townsmen.

Hastings paced the floor restlessly. What motivated Denton was still a mystery. The man had to be insane. Tomorrow countless numbers of people would die, and for what? To satisfy a man's vanity? Was Denton striking out for what he imagined had happened to him at some time? The whole thing was so incredibly impossible. Hastings understood hatred, and vengeance was something that had nearly consumed him. In a way he was guilty of the very same things he was laying at Denton's door. Not on the same scale, perhaps, but hadn't he killed often in the past twenty years, and for what reason? Because he had permitted hatred and vengeance to rule his life. Well, it was too late to do anything about that now. Besides, it was more important that he alert the people who stood in Denton's way on the morrow.

He had to get out of the guardhouse, find a way to rescue Margaret, and get both of them outside and into town. He examined the door. It was constructed of rough-hewn, squared-off timbers, snuggly fitted together. The door was hung with large iron hinges which he couldn't hope to pry off from the inside. The lock was situated within the door so it could be locked from either side. That knowledge did him little good, since he had no key nor anything he could use to pick the lock. Even if he managed that somehow, he was sure he remembered a bar on the outside in addition to the lock. The door was out of the question.

He examined every square inch of the floor, but it was uniformly hard. It would be like digging through a slab of solid rock. After a careful inspection of the walls, he could see that there was no possibility there either. They were surprisingly well-fitted together. Only a minimum amount of hard-clay chinking had been used to stop the gaps between the logs. The bark had been stripped from them and it appeared that considerable labor had been expended, so that they joined in nearly perfect fashion. He slammed his fist into his palm. Cursing, he kicked at the pallet. This wouldn't do. Calm was needed now.

The roof! Why hadn't he thought of it before? Standing on tiptoe and scaling the walls soon proved fruitless. The roof of the cell was as escape-proof as the rest of the guardhouse. The only other thing was to somehow overpower the guard and his keys. All he needed was some ruse to get the guard inside. No, that wouldn't work either. Each time the door had been opened there had been at least two armed soldiers present in addition to the guard. No doubt, this was a precaution they took with any prisoner. Giving up for the moment, he decided to wait for darkness before he tried anything. His chances of success would be much greater under the cover of darkness.

18

The hours dragged, and his impatience grew with each passing moment. On several occasions he had been tempted to try some trick on the guard in hopes that he could walk out. Each time he fought back the urge, but not without great difficulty.

After an eternity the light that filled the small window faded to black. From his position on the floor he could see stars twinkling in the sky above. No clouds—good! Clouds produced brighter conditions at night. He was thankful for the star-lit sky devoid of moon—devoid at least until much later.

Searching his memory he tried to recall what time they had changed guards the night before, but he couldn't remember. He fished his watch out of a vest pocket, but the interior of the cell was so dark he couldn't make out the face let alone the time. There had been no change since suppertime, so it should come soon.

After what seemed like hours, he heard voices just outside the door, and his heart leapt into his throat. Excitement surged through him. Two men talked in low voices. One laughed; then more clearly they bade one another goodnight.

He forced himself to wait—five, ten, fifteen minutes.

He moved cautiously over to the window and peered out. His vision was good due to the darkness of his cell and the comparatively lighter courtyard. The lights in the house were burning, and he could see one window on the second floor near the front which was alight. That must be Margaret's room.

The guard on the front gate was visible as he walked along the elevated platform that passed over the top of the gate and extended thirty yards to either side. The guard outside of his cell was a tall, slender fellow who now stood leaning against the door with his right leg bent at the knee and his foot braced against the door. Hastings saw that by stretching his arm through the window he could easily reach the guard's coat collar.

On impulse he thrust his arm through the opening and grabbed the guard's collar and pulled the man up sharply against the door. Momentarily, the guard was off balance and could not free himself. Realizing that he could hold him thus for only a few more seconds, he quickly worked his neckerchief from around his own neck and deftly wrapped it around the neck of the guard. Holding the ends in opposite hands he pulled them tight, garrotting the hapless victim. The man struggled. His convulsions ended and he sagged limply, becoming a dead weight in the make-shift noose that he had fashioned.

Holding the ends of the neckerchief still twisted tightly around the guard's neck with his left hand, he sought to reach the keys on the guard's belt with his right. It was an awkward position because he could get his arms only part way through the window. Exerting all of his remaining strength he pulled back on the twisted piece of cloth and reached his right arm through the small opening, fishing blindly with his fingers for the keys. His fingertips touched the keyring clipped to the guard's belt. Just then he felt a tearing pain shoot through his left shoulder. The man slipped from his weakening grasp and fell limply to the ground.

A rush of warm blood seeped down his back. He had reopened the wound and he did not have the keys. In time they would find the dead guard, and he would be forced to follow in Slater's footsteps. His shoulder throbbed unbearably, and he couldn't stop the flow of blood. He kicked at the pallet viciously and denied an urge to snatch it up and rip it into shreds. "Oh, my God!" he sobbed in a half whisper. I've got to remain calm, he reminded himself in the next breath. Going to pieces will gain nothing now.

He was about to sit again when he remembered the knife in his boot. They had missed it when they had searched him earlier. He pulled it out of its hidden sheath and hefted it. It was too light to dig with, especially in this hard floor. Perhaps, it could be used as a lock pick, but he doubted that it was strong enough for even that. Another idea came to him, and he sank to his knees and began to cut the canvas cover of his pallet into long thin strips. Sweat, coming more from his attempt to endure the pain than from the exertion of ripping the canvas to pieces, covered his brow and soaked his shirt. One strip, about six-feet long, he tied to the knife at the point of balance. Getting to his feet, he wiped the perspiration from his forehead. Moving swiftly to the window he dropped the knife outside. He raised and lowered it until he heard the distinct 'tink' of metal on metal. Maneuvering the knife until it caught in the ring, he hoisted the cloth, pulling the knife up with it. It snapped up all at once as the knife slipped out of the ring.

Patiently, he continued to fish with the knife. He lost count of the times he had felt the knife catch, only to spring free a second later. His patience ebbed, and his frustration grew. A desire to hurl the knife earthward and to tear the door apart with his bare hands came. At this point he stopped his fishing and tried to gather his wits.

After resting for a few minutes he went back to work. Finally, the knife caught tightly, and he lifted it gently, holding his breath for fear the ring of keys would fall from his grasp. The ring was at the edge of the window. Carefully, he extended his right hand, clutched the keys and drew them inside. At last he knew the sweetness of success. Panting and out of breath, he nervously fitted the keys one after another into the lock until he found one that turned. Sighing deeply, he pushed gratefully at the door. It wouldn't budge! He gritted his teeth, gnashing them together frantically. He had forgotten the bar!

He reached his arm out through the window, and found by stabbing down as hard as he could with the knife that the point would catch and he could move the bar a few inches until the point of the knife came free of the wood. Agonizing minutes passed. Again and again he struck with the knife. Finally, it held and he edged the bar out of the bracket. The door gave all at once, and swung open. With his weight pressed against it, he went stumbling out into the courtyard, sprawling on the ground. He lay still for a while, until his breathing went back to normal. He jerked the pistol from the guard's holster and shoved it into his own. As an extra precaution he fumbled a handful of extra shells out of the guard's belt and dropped them into his shirt pocket.

Glancing at the guard on the front gate, he knew he'd have to stay put until the guard was walking the other way with his back toward him. The guard walked to the near end of his platform, turned and started back the other way. Hastings crouched, waited until the guard was about half way through his trip to the other end, then made a dash for the back of the stable. The least exertion brought pain to his shoulder and his strength was slowly draining out through the hole in his back.

He moved slowly along the back of the stable. Carefully, he edged a rear door open and slipped inside. A flickering light came from the other end, and he could hear muffled voices. Four of Denton's soldiers were seated on bales of hay with a fifth bale in the center serving as a table. They were playing cards, and every once in a while a bottle appeared and made the rounds.

Hastings found his black in an end stall. He edged into the stall, quickly clapping his hand over the horse's muzzle to prevent an unwanted whicker. While he talked soothingly to the animal, he heard a clatter of hooves approach the stable from the direction of the front gate. A moment later a voice called out, "Fletcher, I'm back. Take care of my horse."

"Yes, sir," Fletcher answered, but made no move to obey the order.

Hastings finished saddling the black. The voice was familiar and an image of its owner came to him. Burton! That meant both Denton and Burton would be in the house. It could complicate his getting Margaret out safely. She had to have a horse. They couldn't ride double and get away from any pursuit that might follow. He glanced along the row of stalls. The next two were empty. The third was within the circle of light emanating from the lantern used to light the card game. If they were lucky Burton's horse would go into one of these stalls. Of course, if Fletcher brought the horse back in he would see that Hastings' horse was saddled. Well, he couldn't worry about that now. He'd have to take his chances.

He went back out the door he had entered through, staying close to the stable wall for as long as he could. At the end of it he paused and waited until the guard on the front gate was in just the right position—then he ran, hunched over, until he reached the back porch of the house. He was gasping, sucking in great lungfulls of air so deep that it pained him. His strength ebbed more rapidly, and he felt dizzy. The surroundings blurred, and he sat down, holding his head in his hands, until he felt strong enough to go on.

The back door opened easily. Inside, he found he was in a large kitchen. There were cupboards along the wall, cooking utensils hanging from nails driven above the sideboard. A large iron stove occupied nearly the whole of one wall. There was only one other door. Opening it he found himself in a long hallway. The hall floor was covered with a long, hooked rug. There was a door on his left, and he could see the front door at the other end of the hall. Between him and the front door were two more doors both on his left. From the nearer one came the sound of voices and the flickering of lamp light. On his right were the stairs, leading up to the second floor. He moved far enough down the hall to enable him to look into the lighted room. Denton and Burton were studying a map. Had they missed the one Margaret had smuggled to him?

He went back to the stairs and climbed slowly. Each creaking board sent his heart racing. Apparently, the two below were too engrossed in what they were doing to hear the creaking stairs. Perhaps, too, the noises weren't as loud as they seemed to him. About half way up the stairs, he felt a wave of dizziness, and he clutched the railing tightly to keep from falling. At the top of the stairs he found another corridor with doors leading from it. Recalling the light in the front window .earlier, he gambled that the far door led to Margaret's bedroom. He tiptoed down the hall. The door was locked! He glanced back down the stairs. What if their meeting ended suddenly? Well, everything was a gamble. There was no stopping now. He removed his knife from its sheath and slipped the blade between the door and the jamb. By twisting first one way, then the other, while forcing the knife upward, he was able to force the lock. He eased the door open and stepped inside. There was a form on the bed. Moving closer he touched a shoulder.

"Margaret," he whispered. "Margaret, wake up."

She stirred. "Bret! Oh, Bret. How did you get out?"

"Never mind now," he whispered. "We've got to get out of here quick!"

She rose. Her clothes were twisted and wrinkled. They walked to the door.

"When we get outside, you go over to the stable, stay along the back, and go in the back door. My horse is in the last stall. Burton's horse may be in the next stall or it may still be outside. Bring the horses to the back gate. Be careful! There are four men playing cards in the stable. You'll have to be quiet. If either horse is unsaddled bring it anyway. Don't bother with a saddle. You okay?" She nodded.

"While you're doing that, I'll take care of the guard at the back gate."

She disappeared safely behind the stable, and he cautiously stalked the man guarding the back gate. Crouching, he crept up behind the unwary man, clasped his left hand over the man's mouth, and in the same motion brought the blade of the knife across his throat. He held him upright until the man ceased to quiver, then he let him drop. Margaret came out of the darkness, leading two horses—both with saddles. The negligent Fletcher had not yet carried out his order. A noise echoed from the direction of the house! He spun around just in time to see Burton come off the porch yelling, "Hey, what's goin' on over there?"

Before he reacted a tongue of flame issued out of the darkness and his arm was smashed with a numbing impact. The force twisted him half around, and sharp

189

pain roared through him. He stumbled, found his balance, clawed for his pistol, jerked it clear and fired. Burton doubled up and pitched forward. Waiting no longer he ran headlong to where Margaret stood, and with great difficulty managed to get himself into the saddle.

"Let's ride!" They raced their horses through the back gate with sounds of chaotic turmoil reverberating behind them. He clung desperately to the saddlehorn with his right hand, pitching dizzily to and fro in the saddle, his left arm dangling loosely. The bullet fired in the dark had shattered the bone.

19

They rode hard, pushing the horses to the limit, but there was no sign of pursuit.

"Who can we talk to in town?" he asked. He felt weak and faint. "It's got to be someone who can go to the people with what we've got to report."

"Eb Morley, I guess," she answered. "He's president of the town council. He's the oldest of the Morley brothers who own the Emporium, the store where we ran into each other that day so long ago." She looked away, squeezing tears from her eyes.

They rode along Main Street with intentions of crossing the river to reach Morley's home which was down the left fork in the road that led to the Grahams' place. As they passed the Emporium, Hastings glimpsed a light showing from the back. Maybe Morley was still at the store, catching up on some work or other business. They pounded on the door, waited and pounded some more. Finally, Morley heard them, came across the darkened store, and opened the door.

"Hastings! What happened? My God, Mrs. Denton, what has happened?" Morley was frightened—frightened of the tattered, bloody figure which stood before him.

"We got into a little set-to," Hastings said. "There ain't

time to explain. We've got to talk to you—right now!"

"Well, ah...certainly. Ah...won't you come in. We had a council meeting tonight. I was just finishing up some business," Morley explained as he stepped aside to allow them to enter.

Hastings could sense the man's uneasiness. Once inside Morley's office, Hastings told him all he knew of Denton's plan.

Morley, somewhat more at ease, thought about what Hastings had said. "I'll tell you what, I'll go get the town council members. I think they're still over at the Bonanza—most of them, anyway. You tell them what you told me. You wait right here, I'll be right back." He left in a rush, obviously relieved to be out of the place.

Margaret touched Hastings' sleeve. "You need a doctor, Bret. I'm going to get Dr. Loring."

He smiled down at her. "Okay, Margaret, I reckon everything will be all right now." At last it's over, he thought.

She left. Five minutes crawled by, then he heard bootheels coming across the store toward the office. He started to get up from the chair but found he was too weak to rise. Morley came in accompanied by Carlyle and a towheaded boy of about seventeen, toting a shotgun.

"There he is, Marshal," Morley said, pleased with himself.

Carlyle, the jailer, was now the acting marshal, and he had a kid for a deputy. Hastings wasn't surprised.

"On yer feet, Hastings, you are under arrest—and this time you ain't gonna get out of it."

Hastings struggled to his feet and preceded the grinning marshal out of the store and down the boardwalk to the marshal's office.

Once he was safely locked in the cell, Carlyle addressed him, grinning broadly. "Sleep well, Hastings. We is gonna

192

hang you in the mornin'. Keep an eye on him, Michael," he said to the kid. "I'll see you early in the mornin'." He dropped his greasy, sweat-stained hat on a wall peg and stretched out on a cot at the far end of the marshal's office, and almost immediately he was snoring loudly.

20

Sleep was impossible in the cramped, dingy cell. Hastings' shattered arm lay useless at his side, throbbing with almost unendurable pain. The wound in his back added to his torment, and he was physically weak from loss of blood. With Tuck dead and Jed missing, there was no help—no way of getting to Denton. His will was gone along with any hope of escaping the carnage that Denton's Army would bring on the morrow. What the hell was the use? he thought. I've done all any man could do.

Time drifted. A muffled murmer of voices issued from beyond the door, emanating from the office. Hastings couldn't identify the words spoken, let alone the identity of their speakers. More than likely it was the kid and Carlyle gloating over their prisoner. Well, he couldn't really blame them. They were doing their job.

Presently, the oaken door swung open, and a shaft of yellow light speared down the narrow corridor and into his cell. He tried to rise but could only manage to turn his head toward the door. The kid was leading a very large man—a man so fat that he had trouble negotiating the constricted passageway—along the hall toward his cell. The kid inserted a key into the lock, twisted it one way, then the other, swung the door open, and stepped aside to allow the fat man to enter. The latter waddled into the cell. Hastings sat up on the hard bunk. The kid closed and locked the door behind the fat man and stood back, cradling a shotgun like a baby in his arms.

"Howdy, Hastings. I'm Doc Hedgepeth."

Hastings' mind tripped nimbly over a series of recent events. He should know this man. There were only two doctors in the area, and this one wasn't Dr. Loring.

"You're Denton's surgeon, aren't you?"

"Was," the Doctor corrected. "I quit him! That wasn't easy, but it was time. I guess a culmination of events over the years made me look at myself,—but it was you and your narrow escape awhile ago that finally jarred my senses into the proper perspective. Let me look at that arm." He took the injured arm in his pudgy hands. Soft, blunt fingers tenderly explored the injury. Hastings winced.

"Broken," he muttered, "but you lost the bullet. Hey, boy," Doc called.

The kid stepped forward, leveling his shotgun.

"Get me some water and a broomstick or a mop, whichever you have in there. Oh, yes. Some whiskey if you have it."

"Broomstick . . . mop handle?" The kid looked puzzled. "What fer?"

"Never you mind. Do as I say. Now get a move on!"

"Here," Doc said, digging into the waist of his trousers. He produced a small, double-barreled derringer—one barrel above the other. "I never could use this myself and I'm not sure it will be of use to you in your condition, but it's all I have to offer. Fixing that arm and this toy is about all I can do for you. I'm a coward, boy. I quit Denton all right but I'm not wasting any time getting away from here. I'm going back to St. Louis. I think I can leave the

195

whiskey alone now and maybe I can be a doctor again if I work at it. I'm going to give it a try anyway. There was a time when I was a good doctor."

Hastings slipped the tiny gun under his belt. Doc went to work on his arm. "Has Denton started for town yet?" he asked. He wanted to give it all up—let whatever was to come, come; but deep down an ember of the old hatred still glowed.

"No, I think he'll wait until daylight. There is nothing to stop him now. I guess you were it, boy, and you didn't measure up. Not that any one man could. You came close, though. My advice to you is to use that toy to get out of this cell, then ride out of here while there's still time. Take Margaret with you. Denton knows you and he'll be looking for you come morning."

"Where is Margaret?"

"She's fine, boy. I saw her over at the hotel. She sent me over here. I tried to get her to go with me when I leave, but she wouldn't hear of it. She's a good woman, boy—a mighty good woman."

The kid returned sans shotgun, carrying a broom and a mop in one hand and a bucket of water in the other with a bottle of whiskey tucked under his arm. He handed the broom, the mop, and the bottle between the bars to Doc, one at a time. Doc opened the bottle and took a long drink and handed it to Hastings.

"That'll settle my nerves," he said, wiping his mouth with the back of his hand.

Hastings tilted the bottle and drank until he retched and tears flowed down his cheeks. He gritted his teeth and drank more whiskey until his mind was fuzzy. Doc hefted the broom and mop—one in each hand—and selected the broom and took out a large pocket knife. He made two circular grooves with the knife, one above the broom head and the other half-way between this cut and the end. He broke off the head, then broke the handle in half,

196

trimming the rough edges with the knife. He fitted the sticks along Hastings' arm, making sure the bone was still in place, and wrapped them there with bandages he produced from his bag.

"That'll do you if you don't get too active. You might have Dr. Loring look at it in a couple of days . . . if you are still around that is." He began to gather his things together in preparation to leave.

"Thanks, Doc . . . for everything," Hastings said as the kid opened the cell door.

"Think nothing of it. I wish I could do more, but, well . . ."

"Good luck in St. Louis."

Doc nodded and waddled down the hall and disappeared through the door. Hastings lay back. The pain was constant but not as intense as before. His mind was clouded by the alcohol, and the bottle was on the floor. A few more drinks and all the pain would be gone. He reached for the whiskey, then drew back. A sense of complete futility overwhelmed him and he almost laughed at the ridiculousness of the situation. He had a two-shot derringer with which to stand off an army, and he was so badly hurt he could hardly sit up—and he was in jail to boot.

Hastings slept in snatches, dozing off, then waking as the pain fluctuated like short tides, coming and going. At dawn he arose and worked the kinks out of his stiff, sore muscles. Time was growing short, and he knew he must make a move soon. Denton would be on his way in, and he had to do something! Anything would be better than waiting here. He fished the derringer out of his belt and palmed it against his thigh.

"Kid," he called.

The youth appeared instantly, cradling the shotgun as before, his eyes red with lack of sleep.

Hastings showed him the derringer.

197

"Hand me that shotgun—stock first. Don't make any sudden moves. I don't want to shoot you, son, but there's more at stake than your life or mine!"

The boy was terrified, his young mouth hung agape, and his eyes were staring widely as he did what he was bid. Fear had made the shotgun a worthless instrument to the kid.

"Now, open that door and be quiet about it. I wouldn't want to disturb Carlyle's sleep just yet."

Once outside the cell he nudged the boy inside.

"Sit tight," he said, and stepped into the office, roused Carlyle and ushered him into the cell along with the boy.

"You'll never git away, Hastings. Ever'body is lookin' to hang you."

Hastings looked at Carlyle. He felt sorry for the old man—being locked in his own jail would destroy what was left of his pride. He pushed through the oaken door, securing it behind him. He discarded the shotgun and rummaged through the desk drawers until he found a pistol. After checking the loads he slipped it into his empty holster and stepped into the street.

Denton, riding at the head of a double column of forty men, the old sergeant directly behind him, was just passing the first of the town's buildings and riding slowly in Hastings' direction. Moving into the middle of the street, he was intent on forcing a confrontation. His bandaged left arm hung stiffly at his side.

The curious were starting to line the boardwalk. Heads could be seen at most of the upstairs windows, and a number of people had grouped along both sides of the street.

It was early for so many people to be about. They must have somehow sensed the coming showdown. Of course, they could have seen the army coming down the ridge west of town and gathered here to watch whatever was to come. He eyed them—these people who knew nothing of what was in store for them. He didn't know what he was going to do, so he would just have to play it as it came.

Denton rode to within twenty feet of him and dismounted. The troops halted behind him without a command. He took two steps forward, facing Hastings. His boots shone, his uniform was creased and wrinkle-free. His hat was set squarely on his head, and he seemed no different now than he had so many years ago. The same perfection of appearance and manner, the same strange light burning behind his eyes.

"We meet again, Hastings. I suppose I should have killed you that last time but I never dreamed you would blame me for the actions of that whore of a mother of yours."

Hastings heard the words, which were meant to provoke him but they meant nothing to him now. He almost felt ready to agree with Denton. Why was he here now? Why did he need to face this man? The worthless years he had spent seeking to avenge the wrongs done him were nothing more than that—worthless. His life had been wasted on a useless crusade and now he must die. It would be over soon and despair filled him—then he realized something was wrong! The calm-cool feeling was strangely eluding him. Could he fight without it? He glanced at Denton. A stab of fear penetrated his heart, and his good hand was shaking. He had always thought he would welcome death. Now, he was afraid to die. Terror of the man before him was consuming him. For so long he had waited to meet him face to face. Fear was a new feeling; a feeling he could not remember experiencing before. His left arm was numb, and he was frozen in place. He had to think, to clear his head of the freezing fear that gripped him.

"Hastings, you've sought me for some twenty-odd

years, seeking vengeance you think is just. Therefore, I will give you the opportunity to satisfy your craving for revenge. You may think you are good and you may well be, but you will have to be the fastest of the fast to take me, and I say that in all modesty. I don't boast."

Hastings continued to tremble. All that he knew, and all that he had heard of Denton verified what the man said. Of the many things Denton might be, one thing he was not—a braggart. He waited. Denton waited. Horses pawed impatiently, and soldiers shifted in their saddles uncertainly. Should I make the first move, or should I wait for him to draw first?

"I see you haven't the courage to draw first, and I won't give you any satisfaction by being first," Denton said. "Sergeant, count to three!"

"One," Hastings heard the Sergeant rasp. "Two... three!"

Denton's movement was a blur, as Hastings reached for his gun. His fingers tightened on the grip, and the gun stuck! His hand slipped away. An explosion rocked the early morning air, and he heard a bullet whiz by his ear. He clutched at the gunbutt, and this time the gun jerked free. Another shot roared. A stinging numbness struck his hand as his gun sailed out of his grip, hopelessly out of reach. Denton fired again. The bullet smashed into his shoulder inches above his heart. The pain blinded him, and the impact whirled him around. Black dots danced before his eyes as his vision cleared. He tried to catch himself as he fell, hoping to avoid falling on the injured arm. A second later, excruciating pain wracked his being as he heard the crude splint snap under the weight of his body.

Pain lulled his senses, and his body relaxed, demanding a cessation of activity. He couldn't take any more punishment. If only he could just lay there and die, but blind instinct sent him into action. Using all of his remaining strength, he rolled over as another bullet kicked dust into his face. Frantically, he reached for the derringer in his belt. He pointed the small gun at Denton and with a super effort, requiring the last of his ebbing strength, he managed to fire the little pistol, squeezing both triggers at the same time. Denton's face vanished in a splash of red just before his own face crashed senselessly into the dust of the street.

21

Strange images flitted across Hastings' mind. John Denton's face drew near, expanded like an inflating balloon, then exploded, noiselessly, in a gusher of red fluid. Out of the sea of red came a brown-clad army, infinite in number, riding their mounts at full charge. The rearing horses surged over him one at a time, trampling him unmercifully into the dust. The excruciating pain of each stamping hoof smashed against his defenseless body, mutilating it beyond repair. Among these mirages of the mind, he could, at times, see Margaret's worried face floating evasively in a gray mist. Her ghostly image was always accompanied by a dark-bearded face he didn't recognize. Then came the blankness—the periods which brought only blackness to his mind's eye, and nothing registered on his conscious mind. Again and again the images came and went, separated by eras of nothingness. Blurred wavy patterns of light, distorted into zig-zags of muted color, were followed by thin rainbows of light carrying a bearded face he had seen so often before.

This time the bearded man was alone. He tried to grasp consciousness—to pull himself out of the world of twisted light and black, and back into the real world. The stranger's face faded from his focus, then sharpened again, faded once more, then again sharpened into focus. The light patterns rearranged themselves, gradually taking on the appearance of a room and its furnishings.

Hastings found himself in bed, swathed in bandages. A nagging hurt was present in every segment of his body.

The strange bearded face he had seen in his dream world belonged to a small man, slight of build and filled with nervous energy. The man wore pin-striped pants and a vest to match. His ferret face was crowned with thinning, sandy-colored hair. On his nose was perched a pair of steel-rimmed glasses. He approached the bed.

"Ah, Hastings. You are finally awake?"

"I seem to be. What happened? Where's Denton?"

He ignored Hastings' questions and proceeded to poke and probe his body, occasionally stopping to listen with a stethoscope.

"I think you'll be fine after a while. It's only a matter of time now. I'm Dr. Loring, by the way. There are several people waiting to see you. If you feel up to it, I'll tell them it's all right for them to come in for a while."

The Doctor left, and Margaret entered, followed by Jed, Laurie and Eb Morley. Margaret perched on the bedside. The others positioned themselves near the foot. Margaret leaned over and kissed his cheek. He grinned in return. Jed drew a look of utter amazement. The old man was dressed in a suit, complete with a fancy vest. His bald head was topped with a derby hat, and a colorful cravat was knotted at his throat. He was clean-shaven and he had recently had his hair trimmed.

"You're going to be all right now, Bret," Margaret said, drawing his attention from Jed.

"What happened, Margaret? I don't remember. Is John...?"

"John is dead," Margaret said with no trace of remorse in her voice. "You shot him, and he died in the street before he could kill you. You gave us some anxious moments though." She wrinkled her nose at the unpleasant thought.

"I hit him in the face, didn't I?"

Margaret nodded. "It wasn't pretty, but he was going to kill you, and maybe everybody in town. He had to die, Bret. There was no other way." Her eyes were dry. There was no outward sign of sadness over her husband's death. In fact, she was making excuses for him.

"But his army, why didn't they react?"

"We'll never know for sure," Morley said. "That old Sergeant—what's his name—O'Brien, isn't it? He gave those men a command as soon as Denton was hit, and he saw to it they marched straight out of town. We haven't seen any of them since. It would seem that Denton's Army has ceased to exist."

Silence pervaded the room. Morley looked about from face to face, then he stepped forward, twisting his hat brim around and around in his hands.

"Mr. Hastings." He paused as if trying to work up his courage. His head was bowed, and he was avoiding Hastings' searching eyes.

"We—the town, and me most of all—owe you an apology. We wronged you, but you stuck it out and set us free of the yoke Denton had around our necks. For all of us I'm saying we are truly sorry." He looked up, awaiting Hastings' reaction.

"It's okay, Mr. Morley. I hung on for reasons other than just the town. I'm glad everything worked out so well."

"One more thing," Morley said. "The town council has asked me to . . . well . . . we want you to be our town marshal when you are able to be up and around. Would you honor us by accepting the position?"

"Well, Mr. Morley, I'll take the job providin' two conditions are met."

"What are they? Well, whatever they may be, I'll do what I can to see that you are satisfied."

Hastings laughed. "I reckon you can only meet one of 'em, Mr. Morley. First," he said, drawing it out purposely, "I'll consent to takin' the job if Margaret won't mind bein' a marshal's wife." He looked hopefully at Margaret. "I know it's a bit soon to be askin' for your hand, but—"

Margaret flushed. "Oh, Bret. I'd love to be a marshal's wife if you are the marshal." She leaned over and kissed him on the lips. Then becoming aware of the others watching her, she drew back, her face reddening in embarrassment.

Hastings grinned up at her. The feeling was wonderful despite the pain. Jed had a lopsided grin spread across his face.

"What are you all duded up for?"

Jed grinned back at him, tucked his thumb under his lapel and patted his derby hat.

"Yuh like this here outfit? Laurie picked it out fer me. I'm agoin' tuh carry her back to Georgie. She's got people back there. I reckon that's whur she belongs right enough."

"I agree," Hastings said, looking at Laurie. She smiled in return, but even the smile couldn't erase the lines of sadness about her eyes. Her life in the West had been a trying ordeal, and he hoped she'd forgiven him for his part in it. Undoubtedly, she'd stand a better chance of finding happiness back East.

Jed said, "I figgered iffen I was agoin' to hobnob with city fellers I damn well better look like 'em!"

"Er...excuse me, Mr. Hastings," Morley said. "Would you tell me the second conditon for your taking the marshal's job? I have to report to the town council, you know."

"That's right. I didn't mention it did I?" He paused.

"Well, if I'm to be marshal of Northgate I want Jed Bannock for my chief deputy. That is, if he don't stay back East. I reckon a fellow could find city livin' mighty easy after knocking about on the plains all his life."

"Damn yer hide, Bret Hastings. Soon's I get this here gal settled back East, I'll be back here tuh see you do that there town marshal's job right. Me a livin' in a city! Hell, yuh know me betterin' that."

"Looks like we got ourselves a marshal," Morley said. "I'll report to the town council at once." He left the room triumphantly.

Jed fished a large gold watch out of his vest pocket. "Looks like this here gal and me has got tuh git. We got a stage tuh board. I'll expect tuh see yuh up and around, atotin' a sixgun when I git back."

"So long, old timer. Bye, Laurie."

She looked at him for a long time. "Thanks for everything, Bret. You get well real quick, and I hope you and Margaret will be real happy." She looked at Margaret and the two women embraced tearfully.

"If you ever come back to Georgia, you two, be sure to come and visit me."

"We will be sure and do that," Margaret said. She accompanied them to the door and closed it after they had left.

She perched on the bedside and clasped his hand in hers.

"It's all over now, Bret. It was all so horrible, and I'm so happy!"

"Yeah, the bad days are over. The good life is just beginning."